My Dead World 3

JACQUELINE DRUGA

VULPINE PRESS

My Dead World 3 by Jacqueline Druga

Copyright © 2019 Jacqueline Druga

Published by Vulpine Press in the United Kingdom in 2019

ISBN 978-1-83919-004-9

www.vulpine-press.com

Also by Jacqueline Druga:

No Man's Land

When Leah and Calvin found out they were expecting, they were over the moon. That day would be one to remember forever... but for more reasons than one. That was the day the world changed. That was the day joy turned to fear. A deadly virus broke out, with many of those infected becoming violent and uncontrollable. And it was spreading fast.

The Last Woman

After emerging from a coma, Faye Wills opens her eyes to complete darkness and the feeling of being trapped. She awakens in the worst place imaginable, one of thousands of bodies in a makeshift mass grave that was once a football stadium.

Left for dead, there are no signs of life and the only sound she hears is the buzzing of flies that follow the stench of death.

Once out of the stadium she steps into a desolate, barren world, void of all life and people. Faye learns that while in a comatose state, the world was besieged by some sort of epidemic. Without a soul around, there are a lot of missing pieces. Where did everyone go?

In her weakened state, she must pull it together and move forward to find answers and survivors. However, she soon realizes that she may never find anyone and must face the possibility that she may be The Last Woman on earth.

ONE

REFLECTION

It never really goes away. That empty feeling, the twinge that hits your stomach the second you think of the person you lost. Even after months, it burns and stings.

I suppose a few months isn't really a lot of time. Certainly not enough time to heal or forget.

It wasn't long after it all started, when my brother gave us that heads-up about the virus.

We prepared. *Hunker down*, he said. Go to the cabin and wait it out.

Waiting it out was laughable.

There is no end to an extinction-level event. You don't wait out anything. Extinction is infinite.

It wasn't too long ago that a young man crashed his car half a block from my home, providing me with the reality check that things were real.

It had begun.

I lost everyone that I loved: my husband, daughter, stepmother, brother, and father.

I was blessed that Katie, my youngest daughter, had beaten the odds. At four years old she has witnessed too much heartache and pain.

It would either define her in life or break her. Though it was too early to tell.

I hated the virus, as everyone else that survived it did.

It infected, changed the person, made them suffer, killed them, and it didn't stop.

On a daily basis we battled abominations of nature. Beings that wanted nothing more than to rip us to shreds.

We did our best to defend ourselves, but in the end we still lost.

Chasing hope was a pipe dream. If we wanted a better life, we needed to find it ourselves. While the world was different, we prayed for a change. That perhaps one day we'd wake up and the madness would be over, and things would go back to the way they were.

Who was I kidding?

I would never again see the day of stopping at a local coffee shop for a quick iced latte.

My days of working job after menial job were done. The job I held now was staying alive and protecting my daughter.

We weren't alone Katie and me. There was a small group of us. Thrown together by circumstances and death. Our shared heartbreak bound us like glue.

We had no real direction, we just followed news we heard over the radio. One person saying they heard this or that.

I had no idea why we were chasing life. Looking for it.

We couldn't be all that was left.

At least alive.

It was a dead world. We all knew it.

Despite how beautiful our surroundings could be—a forest, a lake, a beach—it was overshadowed by a dark cloud of death that would linger for a long time.

One thing was for sure, as time passed, we saw less and less of the dangerous infected.

Those who raged at us, wanting to tear us limb from limb. We went from running and fighting them, to dodging the ones that decayed and barely moved, to not seeing any at all.

But I wasn't so naïve to believe it was over.

It wasn't. Not by a long shot.

We were just at some momentary pause. A calm before the storm. A storm that would eventually slam us.

I wasn't ready.

None of us were.

THE BACK THEN

TWO

CANADA DRY

August 21 – Three Months Post Outbreak

We tried.

More and more, over the radio, speaking to people—an infection-free zone was a reality, we just had to find it.

Like a hamster in a wheel we spun through different phases of emotions on our journey to see the wonderful, undead-free world of Canada. Repeating the emotions every step of the way. Hope, fear, happiness, despair, repeat. When we arrived Canada was, from what we saw, infection free.

The closer we got the less infected we saw.

It was evident they also couldn't take chances and I believed they thought a lot through. Things that never crossed my mind, like children without families. They had an orphan program which was great, until it affected us and they took one of our own. Billy. Billy's parents had been killed, so we took responsibility for him, but it didn't matter. We were informed, like a lost and found object, that if no family crossed over from the United States and claimed him, we could have him back after thirty days.

That was warning one.

They were strict with rules that really made sense. Harsh rules that I agreed with until they applied to us.

No bites.

No exceptions.

To conceal them was a death sentence. Even if the bite mark had never caused an infection. Such was the case with Corbin. He and his son, Sawyer, were part of our group. They'd joined us not long after the outbreak, traveling with two others. They, too, came with Lev, Katie and me to check out Canada while the others stayed behind waiting for a newborn infant to get strong.

Corbin had been bitten months before. His wound had healed, and like Katie, he never turned. Unlike Katie, though, he still got sick. He just beat it.

Why wouldn't the health officials in Canada want him? He, along with my daughter, could be the cure. Or a means to stop it.

Corbin, actually all of us, naïvely believed that his failure to turn into a raging beast was something authorities needed to know.

It was Lev who innocently told doctors about it when they took him to medical. Lev had been shot and had his leg broken. He talked to them about Corbin, something I don't think he'll ever forgive himself over.

When they asked him, Corbin confirmed it never giving it a second thought.

His honesty was met with a bullet.

No delay, no hesitation; the second he showed his scar, a gun was placed to his head. Shot dead in front of my daughter and, even worse, his son.

When they asked if anyone else had been bitten, my daughter said she had, but before they could shoot her Lev went into some sort of protection mode. My gentle giant of a friend went ballistic on the soldier, beating him within a fraction of his life only to be beaten in return within a fraction of his.

They released us because of the action of the callous soldier.

We found ourselves out of Canada, in the middle of the night, in the car we had strategically hidden just in case.

Me, Lev and Katie...not only did they shoot Corbin, they kept his son under their orphan law.

I begged and pleaded, saying he had a grandfather and uncle back in the States that were not far behind.

That didn't matter. The relative would have to make their way to Canada to claim Sawyer.

Sawyer cried and cried, screaming for us. My heart was already broken for Corbin and frightened with how beaten Lev was. Sawyer's cries were salt in an open wound.

Everything crumbled.

Once back in the car, I couldn't go anywhere.

I radioed to tell everyone back at the cabin what had happened. Ben told me what to do for Lev. It was very little and seemed hopeless.

His head was bleeding and he coughed up blood. He could barely keep consciousness.

Ben offered to send Fleck to help but I declined. I would head out at first light.

That was if Lev made it.

My four-year-old daughter was a sobbing mess. Traumatized from watching a man get shot in front of her, then having a gun pointed to her own head.

Had it not been for Lev I would have lost my other daughter, then I would have just died. I would have lied and said I had been bitten so they would shoot me too.

That was hindsight, a horrible hindsight that kept replaying in my mind as I listened to the gurgled breathing of Lev and the constant sobs of my daughter.

There was no comfort to give anywhere.

I gripped the steering wheel with Katie's head on my lap—all I wanted was for the sun to hurry up and rise.

My hands ached, as did my body, and I had to keep it together.

That was a lost cause.

Every time I blinked I heard the shot, saw Corbin fall and Sawyer scream.

Sawyer.

It was hard enough that they had taken Billy, but Sawyer, too? Why hadn't I tried harder, fought more? Instead, I'd just worried about my own, and got out of there as fast as I could, grateful they were releasing us instead of executing us.

I inhaled sharply when I noticed I couldn't hear Lev's gurgled breathing.

"Lev," I called his name, looking into the rearview mirror. "Please Lev, answer me."

It took a few attempts but finally he groaned. I told him to open his eyes, which he did, and for a few moments I could relax, wait out another round of waking him to make sure he was okay.

The hours weren't ticking by fast enough. I thought about leaving anyhow but it was too dangerous, too dark.

Katie was uncomfortable. I knew because she sat up and rolled the other way, leaning against the front passenger door. I double-checked the locks and thought about closing my eyes for a little. Just a little.

I fell asleep, not long or deep enough to dream, but enough for something to happen to my body. My eyes popped open when I felt an enormous wave of nausea hit me. Holding it in, I opened the car door, stepped out and barely made it a foot before the contents of my stomach emptied.

It had to be nerves. Every bit of me shook and I was sick to my stomach.

After shutting the car door, I walked to the back and to the hatch.

It was so quiet, not even the sound of crickets filled the air. Maybe that was the reason I heard it before I smelled it.

Hatch up, reaching in for the blanket, I heard a crunching. Like a foot stepping on something. I would have worried it was someone coming to attack, had I not smelled the scent of rotting flesh.

It wasn't just an infected; it was a nekro, as Edi had named them, meaning they were dead and walking. I knew that because had it been an infected it would have been upon me already. Infected were still alive and moved fast.

Reaching into the hatch, I unzipped our weapon bag containing what we used other than guns to fight with. The first thing I grabbed was a huge wrench.

As soon as my hand touched upon it, I recognized it. It was the one Lev used to put down my husband.

I honed in, listening to the sound of walking and the smell, trying to gauge where he or she was. I knew it was behind me, I just didn't know where. Maybe it had come from one of the cars.

Staying in the glow of the hatch light, I turned around. It took a few seconds to see him, but then I did. He staggered my way, a backpack strapped to him. He moved rigidly, head tilted to the left, his focus on me. He was three car lengths away.

I could have waited for him to come to me, then I worried. Both Lev and my daughter were vulnerable. If something happened to me, the thing would go for them.

I shut the hatch, stayed focused on him and made my way in his direction.

There was no reason for me to feel as brave as I did. None whatsoever, but I did. Not one ounce of fear was present. I didn't know what it was. Was I numb or maybe it was my instinct to protect those I loved? I approached him like I was some sort of pro nekro killer, when I wasn't. I was a great shot, but never one to go hand-to-hand zombie kill mode. Yet, there I was. My hand went flush against his chest to push him back. His shirt was stuck to his flesh and my hand nearly sunk. One push was all it took—he stumbled back some and I struck him in the head. The second I did I knew why I wasn't afraid.

I was too angry.

Too hurt.

Too emotionally broken to even have room for fear.

I wasn't strong enough to do enough damage with that blow. He kind of shucked it off like a cat that had run into a wall, bouncing back my way. I hit him again.

Again, he did the same thing.

Third time was the charm.

I gave it all I had and the wrench impaled the side of his head, sticking there. As he dropped I used the pull of his fall to remove the wrench and then just stared at the thing on the ground. I knew it was down and was no longer a threat, but blinded by such rage, I struck it repeatedly.

It was blind, emotional striking so much that everything was a blur and all I could think of with every hit was someone that I lost. Every hit felt good.

My father, brother, husband...daughter.

Corbin, Edi, Cade...Sawyer.

Slam. Slam. Slam.

No!

On the final blow I dropped the wrench into what remained of his head.

Nothing was left. Nothing.

It was smashed beyond what I believed I was capable of. A thick, slushy pool of nothing.

It wasn't his fault, he just so happened to symbolize the thing that took everything from me.

It was the first time since it all went down that I was out of control.

It was a breakdown, and it was over. At least for then.

I lifted the wrench from the mess, wiped it off on the pant leg of the deader and headed back to the car.

After tossing it back into the weapons bag, I pulled out the pack of baby wipes, shut the hatch, and returned to the driver's seat. I was out of breath and no longer chilled.

It was quiet, sans the sound of Lev's gargled breathing and my daughter's slight whimpering in her sleep. I wiped off my face and hands with the baby wipe, took a drink of water and peered into the rearview mirror.

"Lev, you okay? Lev, get up and answer me. Lev?"

"I'm okay," he replied.

"Thank you." I tossed the baby wipe down and sat back,

My hands were shaking and I watched the skyline for the rising sun.

I just couldn't wait to get out of there.

THREE

STALLED

August 22

"He's not going to die," Ben told me. "But he isn't going to be okay, at least not for a long time. He's got a rough road ahead."

Ben was our godsend. A doctor—a brilliant surgeon—who happened upon our group because he was looking for his son, Brian Cade. Cade had been with us but had died. Ben hadn't wanted to stay after he learned that, but he did. I always believed Lev guilt-tripped him into never leaving.

Good thing for Lev that Ben stayed.

I drove like a bat out of hell from Canada. Faster than I should have and Ben, without even examining Lev, had a clean environment ready in case he had to do surgery. Which ended up being the case. He had to operate to fix the ribs that had punctured Lev's lungs and relieve pressure on his brain.

It was bad. It was really bad.

I don't know how he focused enough to fix Lev, not with all the bad news we brought back with us.

"And Katie?" I asked.

"Katie will be fine. Physically, she is unharmed. Emotionally, she'll heal."

"But she saw things…"

"She has seen things for the last few months," he said. "She is probably the most resilient child I have ever known. She'll have some ups and downs, but she'll get through."

"I'm sorry. I'm sorry about Corbin and Sawyer and Billy."

"Thank you. Fleck tells me that Canada has them in their orphan's program. I would like to go up there and try to get them."

"Absolutely. I'll help in any way I can."

"Good. Good. Because Lev needs more than we have here," Ben said.

"What else can we do?"

"We have that small generator. I would like to go to a nearby hospital—I think Beaver Valley is the closest. I need plenty of IVs, even a pump. I need to give him what he would get if he was in intensive care because that is what he needs."

"He's that bad."

Ben nodded. "He'll make it. He's a tough son of a bitch. He's also the sole reason I have run down on my supplies."

It shouldn't have, but it made me sort of chuckle. It wasn't the first beating Lev had taken. He was still healing from the broken leg and being shot.

"When do you want to go?" I asked.

"As soon as possible. It's still early in the day."

"Beaver Valley. We haven't been that way. I'm not sure what stage the infected are in. But we'll try."

"Fleck can take me. In fact, you're our best shot if something happens."

"Yeah, but I'd feel better with Fleck here. He's a good shot too and he stands a better chance of moving Lev than I do, if need be."

"Agreed. Let me walk Bella through what she needs to do, and if you're up for it, we'll head out."

I nodded, then walked outside to find Fleck.

It was amazing to me that when the whole thing started it was just my family. My father, husband, stepmother and children. We'd gone to the cabin, one we had ready to go, on my brother's advice. It was just us, until we arrived and found Cade had claimed squatters' rights to our cabin. His medical knowledge and immediate reaction to jump and help my husband who had been bitten, sealed him a place in the cabin and in all of our hearts. Lev's family owned the neighboring campground and before long he joined us. But one by one, we died off. Then my brother's arrival was the finishing touch.

Too much to think about, but life gave us another shot. Gave us more people to care about. In a way that sucked, because that was possibly more ways to get emotionally hurt.

Fleck and Bella had joined us right after we had been attacked and removed from our camp. They were with a larger group who were also attacked by the same people. With them was Christina, a young pregnant woman who was injured. Ben delivered her baby boy before she had died. I thought it was ridiculous at first to bring a baby, one who cries, into a world where a single noise could be a death sentence.

They named him Christian, after his mother, and Bella, the teenage girl who was probably reckless and mischievous, took on the role of his mother.

It was good to have them with us. I liked them.

Fleck was a no-nonsense, straightforward person. A bulky guy who had wrestled in an independent circuit. He always wore a bandana on his head. I never saw him without it, so it was hard to say if he was hiding hair or not.

Fleck was a worker, never lazy and was unloading the station wagon when I stepped outside.

"Hey." I walked up to him.

"Hey." He pulled items out from the back. "How's Lev?"

"Stable. Ben and I are gonna take a ride to the hospital to get supplies."

"I figured that was gonna be needed."

"Yeah, so are you okay staying here?" I asked.

"Yeah, you sure you want to go? I mean, you had an ordeal."

"I'd feel better with you here. There's an extra can of gas in the shed if you..." I noticed that Fleck had paused in removing things. "What's wrong?"

He lifted the wrench I had used the night before. It was covered with a dark brownish red substance. I knew what it was.

"Nila, what the hell?" He showed me.

"Don't ask."

"Alright, I won't. I'll get the car ready for you."

I thanked him and told him I wanted to check on Lev and Katie before I headed out again. I was tired and a part of me worried I wasn't in the best shape to make the trip, but I had to.

Katie was awake, sat in the living room on the couch, doodling on a tablet of paper. Her hand moved about seamlessly as she lightly hummed, almost as if she were in a trance.

"Hey, sweetie, how are you?"

"I'm fine, Mommy."

"Do you feel like talking?"

"Nope." She shook her head.

"Honey, I'm going with Ben to get supplies for Lev. Fleck will be here."

"Okay." She looked up to me. "Mommy?"

"Yes."

"Is Lev gonna die?"

"Ben says no."

"He's very bad. He looks bad."

"I know. I take it you have seen him since we got back?" I asked.

17

She nodded with an *a-huh*. "I watched Ben fix him. He put a cut right"—she pointed to her drawing—"there."

The picture, while still on a child's level, was clearly of a bloody Lev.

"I'm drawing so I can show him," Katie said. "Maybe you should take a picture of him so he can see how bad he was."

"Maybe." I mussed with her hair, attributing her attitude to shock and went to the back room where I knew Lev was resting.

When I walked in Ben was speaking to Bella and they both stopped.

"Is he awake?"

Ben shook his head. "He won't be for a while. I'll be ready to go when you are."

"Fleck's prepping the car." I walked to the bed. Lev looked so helpless. His face was swollen, bloodied and bruised, as were both his hands.

He had to get better, he had to.

I quietly said my goodbyes to him, assuring him I'd be back. I didn't know what was out there, infected or not, dangerous or barren, but it didn't matter. It was for Lev. And if it were me in that bed, it wouldn't matter to him either.

FOUR

PICKING

I didn't know very much about anything medical, but I knew my surroundings and the area around the cabin. Corbin and I had previously gone to a veterinary hospital because we didn't want to chance hitting a major hospital—something we ended up doing later, anyhow. It was hard to gauge what was waiting for us, what obstacles, and it was better to stay in rural areas rather than populated. We always had to assume the worst waited for us, and we were usually correct.

This time, though, Ben specifically said a hospital. Beaver Valley.

It was a good hour drive, and while most of it was a highway, I wondered if there was a reason he chose that one.

"I knew about it and saw it when we went to The Green," Ben explained, referencing the safe camp that we had found overrun. "It was pretty accessible when we passed it, no barricades, not a lot of traffic. Why do you ask?"

"Because there's a hospital in Cranberry that would take us half the time to get to."

"Yes, but didn't we determine Cranberry was pretty blocked by traffic?"

"Coming from the city, yes," I replied. "They barricaded that. But when we did the highway, there wasn't much blocking the exits and the area where the hospital is, that's pretty spread out. The hospital is on its own grounds."

"Do you think we'd be able to get close to a door at the hospital? We'll be searching for a lot of supplies. And Cranberry is backtracking."

"Not really backtracking. Maybe a little, but I'm sure," I said. "It's set pretty far back from the road. We'll be able to get to it. That's a lot of grounds to be filled with cars and dead."

"You're sure?" Ben asked.

"Very sure."

And I was.

Then we stopped on the highway. Just before the exit.

I was pointing out where it was and that we could see the hospital from the road, when Ben suggested we pull over and take a look before we get out.

It was a good thing we did.

Where had they all come from?

The usually green grounds that surrounded the hospital were covered with vehicles. All types packed in so tightly that not a spot of grass could be seen. It was if they'd all driven up there trying to get in.

The spaces that *were* between the cars were filled with rotting bodies, or rather the remains of bodies. Worse than that, the dead, the infected that had died, meandered through, bumping into cars, squeezing by, ripping their own flesh from the bones as they did, then reaching down to pick the bones of those already ripped apart on the lawn.

"They're still there," I spoke softly, in shock and in awe.

"Did you think they wouldn't be?" Ben asked.

"Yes. I mean, after Canada, after being up north and not seeing many, I kind of thought or rather hoped…"

"They'd all died off?"

"Yes."

"Ever think maybe Canada cleared a path, killed a whole slew off? And as for them dying off, this thing, dying off, that's really not going to happen. As long as they"—he pointed across to the moving bodies—"are still there."

"That's not true; they can't spread the virus," I said. "A virus needs a living host. They're dead. Cade proved that when he got bit and never got sick."

"Maybe my son was immune like Katie or Corbin," Ben suggested.

I winced. "Oh, no, I don't want to think that. It was such a brilliant theory when Cade said it."

"Alright, we'll stick with the virus needing a living host. But they aren't dead. The blood is still semi-red which means some oxygen remains. It's not coagulating, it's moving."

"There's no heartbeat."

"That you can hear." He exhaled. "Let's get moving. We still have a long drive ahead of us."

I don't know why I had a reluctance to leave at that moment. Part of me wanted to stand there, study what was happening below.

We got back in the car, turned around, and started in the direction of Beaver Valley.

The highway for the most part was clear. Cars stalled on a lane here or there. I wondered why they had stopped, what caused them to do so. I imagined someone in the car that had gone from the sick stage to the infected stage, which happened quickly.

Going from slowly suffering to suddenly wanting to rip someone's throat out.

We made it to Beaver Valley Hospital and while it was nowhere near as crammed with cars, we still couldn't get close enough to the doors without having to walk some distance. It was going to be interesting carrying the supplies and the weapons we'd brought in case we had to fight the infected. Not that we'd brought much. We each had a gun, which we probably wouldn't use because of the noise, and a blunt object. Mine was a tire rod—it rested in the belt of my pants. I would have grabbed the wrench but Ben claimed it first.

Concrete barriers encircled the hospital campus. The lawn and driveway were packed with military vehicles.

"While we were at the cabin," I said, "the world fell apart. But they tried, you know. I could see how hard everyone tried to fight back. What happened? How did we lose?"

"I was on the boat," Ben replied as we walked. "I guess those doing the fighting found they needed to fight for their families and left their posts."

"Can you blame them? We did in our own way. If everyone had stood their ground and fought. If no one had run away, we probably wouldn't be in this mess."

"I wouldn't say that. It got ahead of us before we knew it. I like to believe that someday, somehow, we'll fight for it again. Try to bring it back, you know."

"Ben?" I noticed we weren't walking toward the main hospital building. "Where are we going?"

"We can get what we need there." He pointed to the professional building next to it. "I'm sure of it. I'm also sure the hospital is pretty much, how do you keep saying, *picked over.*"

After a few more feet we stopped. A car was parked against the barrier. It seemed out of place. The front end was smashed, yet it didn't appear to have hit the barrier.

The driver's door was open. No one was inside.

Ben stared at the car.

"What's wrong?" I asked.

"There's no weathering on this car." He turned and pointed to two cars a few feet away. "This car hit those cars to get here." He walked to the car.

"What are you doing?"

After reaching in, he withdrew his hand and rolled his fingers together. "This blood isn't that old."

"Oh, Ben." I reached into my back pocket and pulled out a tiny bottle of hand sanitizer. "Wipe that off."

"Why are you carrying that?" Ben squirted some in his hand.

"Your son."

He smiled slightly. "Next question." He handed the bottle back to me. "Why are you not concerned with what I just said?"

"The blood is fresh. Or close to fresh."

"I think whoever this is came here looking for something."

"Certainly couldn't be for help. No one is here."

"Nila," Ben spoke passively. "If this blood isn't all that old, that means this person was probably bit and if he or she was, that means…"

"Infected."

Ben nodded. "They're somewhere. Be ready."

There really was no way to be ready for an infected. They came out of nowhere and with a vengeance, all we could do was be diligent, eyes open, ears listening.

We could see, when we climbed over the barrier that whoever was injured had done the same. A trail of blood led to smeared bloody handprints on the concrete.

As we approached the door to the professional building, we saw the infected had done the same.

Why the medical building?

Any normal person looking for supplies would go into the hospital

Unless, like Ben, they knew they could get what they needed there. Or, maybe, they knew they were dying and just needed someplace to do so.

23

That was probably wishful thinking and giving the infected far too much credit.

Ben looked inside the building before opening the door. After a beat, we stepped inside.

It was dark with the exception of the light that came in through the windows. The lobby was large with a high ceiling that exposed the entire second floor, and an open staircase leading up. There was a counter desk in the middle directly in front of the elevators.

Ben walked to the directory. "We're in luck. Second floor."

"How do you know?"

"Plastic surgeon—we do a lot of procedures in the office."

As we turned toward the stairs, I heard it.

The all too familiar snarl of an infected.

It was somewhere, I just had to pinpoint where.

I looked one way, Ben another, until I heard the running. Then I knew, it was coming from above.

Just as I looked up, the infected barreled across the second floor directly our way. Only he didn't stop. He ran into the railing and toppled straight over, landing with a thud on the floor not three feet from us.

It only took a second before he jerked, twitched and began to get up.

Ben reached for the wrench and I pulled the rod out.

"I got this," I told him, both hands holding the object as I walked over to the infected while he was still near the floor.

I had every intention of raising it and with all my might, impaling him in the head. In fact, I did those exact motions, but the end of the rod didn't penetrate the skull and the force of the connection vibrated the metal object sending a painful shock into my hands.

"Damn it, why doesn't that work?" I asked, frustrated.

"The skull is a lot tougher than you think." Ben wound back the wrench.

As the infected began to stand, Ben wielded the wrench, cracking him in the back of the head. The infected went down.

"Is he dead?" I asked.

"I don't know. I think." Ben nudged him with his foot.

The infected didn't budge…at first. Then suddenly, he snarled and grabbed onto Ben's leg. Ben, still holding the wrench, nailed him again.

"He is now," Ben said. Using his shoe, he rolled the body over. There was a bite mark across the front of his throat. "Bet this is our car driver." He started to walk away.

"I think we should hit him again."

"Nila…"

"Just to be sure, let's hit him again."

"Be my guest."

I had every intention, and when I raised my tire rod, I looked at him.

His eyes were open but they were lifeless. The familiar black veins created a spider web across his cheek. He was young, maybe in his twenties with darker hair. It was wavy and in that instant, I saw more than an infected.

His eyes were green, they hadn't lost their color yet; his lips were full and parted showing his slightly imperfect teeth

That look right there made me see him…he was human.

He was helpless and had probably been scared in those last moments of his life. The young man on the floor wasn't a monster, he had been sick. He was somebody's child. Some mother out there loved him, wanted the best for him, had worried about him every single second after the outbreak occurred.

It broke my heart for him and for his mother, and I was about to do a repeat performance and desecrate him.

No, I couldn't.

I don't know what happened to me in that second, why suddenly I saw the face of humanity in a being that would tear me apart.

"Nila," Ben called my name.

I hooked the tire rod back onto my belt and before joining Ben, I crouched down and closed the young man's eyes. "I'm sorry for what happened to you."

"Ready?" Ben asked.

"Yeah," I said with a nod and followed him.

That young man was the last surprise guest we saw on the hospital grounds. On the supply run we saw others, some on the road, by cars, some just wandering, but they weren't a threat. We managed to get all the items on Ben's list from the professional building and take it back to the wagon in two trips. As we had time, we also stopped at the Costco. Surprisingly, it hadn't been picked clean.

We'd been away long enough.

For the time being, we had the things we needed. Now Lev needed us so we headed back.

FIVE

TIME BEING

"I had a revelation," I said to Lev. He didn't hear me, or at least didn't acknowledge I had said anything. He hadn't woken up the entire time Ben and I were gone, but on the positive side, Bella said he did stir.

He wasn't going to react, but I wanted to talk to him anyhow.

"Yeah, my revelation. The infected…are people. I know. I know, I can hear you." I did a close Lev imitation. "Nila, we know this, we know they are people, what else would they be?"

I glanced at his steady beeping machine, one that was insanely awkward to move to the car.

"But seriously, Lev, I saw the human being in the infected and it made me feel different. Okay, yes, you probably are thinking all this coming from a woman who poisoned a well in order for forty people to get sick and die. Maybe I'm changing. Who knows? Anyhow, I'll let you rest, I'll be back to sit with you tonight. I really want to be here when you open your eyes." I leaned forward to kiss him on the forehead. "I need to make dinner. And no smart comments."

After adjusting his covers, I left the small room, making my way toward the living area.

Ben was sat on the couch occasionally answering questions my daughter asked while she sat on the floor by his legs drawing. Bella was in the kitchen.

"Where's the baby?" I asked.

"Sleeping," Bella answered.

Then I noticed she was removing items from the cupboards. "Bella, honey, I was coming out to make dinner. Don't worry about it."

Bella froze. She looked at Ben.

"Let the girl make dinner," Ben said. "She's good at it."

"I was going to cook; she doesn't need to do it."

"Again, I'll repeat," Ben said. "Let the girl make diner, she's *good* at it."

"Are you saying I'm not?"

Ben only glanced at me.

"Mommy is a great cook," Katie said

"Thank you, sweetie."

"Everyone else just does better." Katie continued to draw.

I wanted to gasp in shock, but I was realistic. I knew I didn't cook well. The rice was always too hard or too mushy. Things were too salty or bland. It was always one extreme or the other and it wasn't always positive.

Even though it was August it wasn't that hot outside and I told the others I was going to the porch to close my eyes.

Just as I opened the door to leave, Fleck walked in.

"Where are you headed?" Fleck asked.

"Sit on the porch. Bella is making dinner."

"Oh, good, it's not you."

Ignoring his comment I went outside—it had been an insane forty-eight hours. I thought about our journey to Canada, and wondered had we known what it was like, would we still have gone?

The chatter on the radio about going north for life, could we possibly have been the only people who went or had run into trouble. We couldn't have been the only ones that went there with a child orphaned by the circumstances of the world and adopted by a group.

I sat on the porch for a few moments, my eyes so heavy from lack of sleep, yet I couldn't rest. There was something I had to do.

I stood and went back into the cabin.

"You didn't change your mind about cooking, did you?" Fleck asked.

Refraining from any reply, I went into the kitchen and opened up the cabinet where we concealed the radio.

"What are you doing?" Bella asked.

"I don't know if anyone is listening, but on the chance they are," I said, "I need to let them know about the rules of Canada before they head there. Warn them." I lifted the microphone. "It's the least I can do. Because I wish somebody would have warned us."

FIVE

FROM LEV'S SIDE

September 5

When Nila and I were twelve years old, we were always told that we were too big for the playground. I think they meant me. I was a big kid; Nila always seemed to be this bitty thing. Of course, at that age, I was only just starting to grasp the English language.

We would wait until evening to go to the playground. It wasn't to do anything bad—we were our own clique and were still very immature.

We'd run down to the playground and had this dare game. There was a round thing, Nila called it a merry-go-round, but it didn't look like any merry-go-round I had ever seen. It was a large saucer with handlebars for kids to hold while somebody pushed it and made it spin.

Our game was that we would stand on the outside of the saucer, hold on, and run to make it spin to the point our legs lifted from the air. The dare was, who could stand on the outside longer before they jumped on the saucer.

The one particular day we had crushed the ice cream in her father's freezer, consuming every bit, the spinning didn't feel right and I knew that if I didn't stop, not only would I throw up, Nila would be the recipient of it when it carried right back to her. So...I let go.

I was big, I never would have thought that letting go would throw me so far.

It did.

Letting go and sailing was the last thing I remembered.

Until I woke up in the hospital.

Apparently, I landed and hit my head so hard, I fractured my skull.

I wasn't out of it for too long—my father told me only a day—then I was talking gibberish for a day, then after that, I was fine. I had a headache for a while and was warned never to go on that round thing again.

I never did.

I have been told that when a person suffers a head injury, they lose time. They don't remember anything that happened before the injury.

That was not the case when I was twelve and that was not the case of my most recent head trauma.

I remembered everything up until the last blow. The look in that soldier's eyes as I was out of control and pummeling. Never in my life had I felt so enraged. A protective instinct bigger than even I thought I possessed came over me when I saw the gun aim at Katie. I remembered how helpless and pathetic I felt when we sat on the highway waiting for daylight. My head feeling as if there was a knife in it and every part of my body screaming with pain. Nila woke me up constantly. I just wanted to tell her I was sorry for being weak, but the words wouldn't form and eventually I couldn't hold my eyes open.

When I first came to, I was back in Mercy Hospital at twelve years old. I was looking for my father and couldn't figure out why Nila looked so old. At first I thought I had been in a coma for decades, then I remembered...

I remembered.

I guess I had a pattern with head injuries, because when I was trying to speak to her, Nila kept saying, "Lev, honey, I don't understand you."

31

Katie did.

She came to see me when everyone was asleep. She would tell me stories.

Maybe I only spoke gibberish to Nila, or Katie just pacified me.

The pain of that trip to Canada pummeled me more than physically. It wiped me out emotionally. I wished I didn't remember, but I did.

However, I would use the excuse of the head injury to conveniently forget, because I didn't want to talk about it.

We were really back at the cabin safe.

We had failed when we tried to search for The Green, and we failed horribly in our search for an infection-free Canada.

I prayed that, finally, everyone would realize we didn't need to go anywhere. Leaving was a mistake, one I hoped they didn't want to make again.

SIX

AGAIN

September 7

Lev's progress seemed slow. He had finally woken up three days after returning from Canada. His first day awake, I wondered if he had brain damage. He spoke incoherently and looked at us funny for not understanding him.

It didn't take long for him to be alert and speak, well, Serbian. None of us knew what he was saying; I was surprised that he even remembered the language being that he'd traded his native tongue for English when he was ten years old.

He knew who I was, he knew everyone, he just didn't know English.

"It'll come back," Ben told me. "Give it time, it's all part of the head injury."

I remembered when Lev first came to America it took him a long time to learn English. I was a child and it didn't bother me. As an adult, I worried.

Little by little over the next week, his English came back, then so did Lev.

Everything was in a fog to him. It didn't get better. Even after ten days. He recalled Corbin being shot and that was it. He didn't remember beating that soldier or taking a beating.

He did remember an important piece of information though. Canada had ended badly. I was kind of hoping, at least for the time being, that he wouldn't remember Canada at all. That would make my news to him go a little easier.

Fleck and I were going back. We were heading to Canada to try to get Billy and Sawyer.

Lev kept his composure when I delivered the news. "When?" he asked.

"In an hour. We figured we'd head up there and be back either before dark or first thing in the morning."

"You and Fleck?"

"Yeah, Ben wanted to go, but with you still needing watched and the baby…"

"First, I do not need to be watched."

I laughed.

"What's so funny?"

"Not long ago, you were speaking Serbian, Lev. You need watching. You physically can't move the way you need to move. Your broken leg is still healing, plus you went and got yourself pretty beat up."

"But to be babysat."

"I know this is a lot for you," I said. "I get it. I do. But if you don't heal right, you'll never be a hundred percent and I need you a hundred percent. Understand?"

Lev nodded.

"We'll keep in touch by radio…" I snapped my finger. "Speaking of which. I spoke to Hal on the radio."

"It's been a while."

I nodded. It had been. We hadn't heard from Hal since before our cabin was attacked and not talking to him made us all believe he had either been attacked himself, or had been in on the hit we took.

"What did he say?" Lev asked.

"He was headed to Canada. I told him about the rules. He was fine with them, he just needed to get to an infection-free area."

"It's so dangerous out there, Nila."

"I know. But Fleck and I will be careful. I know the route to take that's pretty clear. It'll take us right up to the border road."

"But what was clear two weeks ago, may not be clear now."

"We'll try. We'll avoid getting close to Buffalo as there were a lot of infected there. After that, you know it was pretty clear."

"I'm allowed to be concerned," Lev said.

"You are. I am too, mainly," I said. "What the hell am I going to talk about to Fleck for five hours?"

I thought it was funny. Lev didn't.

He still wasn't himself, and still not feeling well, I could tell. Sick or not, I knew he understood going to Canada again was something we had to do.

"Burgers," Fleck said. "I miss burgers."

"We could make venison burgers," I said. "Not the same but close." Then I cringed. What was I doing? I was perpetuating the food conversation that seemed to have taken up most, if not all, of the ride. That was what Fleck wanted to talk about.

Food.

Why?

Talking about things like pizza and tacos was only going to make it worse.

"Maybe they have them in Canada," Fleck suggested.

I didn't think we were going to be there long enough to get takeout. I tried to explain to Fleck what we'd see. How after Buffalo,

35

we'd hit that scenic route until the roadblock at the border, and then from there we'd have to walk. We'd see very little if any infected or deaders.

Deaders was a name Corbin had given those who had been infected, then died and kept going. That was the one thing, other than food, that we talked about. For Corbin we would forever call them deaders.

It really looked like I was going to hold true to my word. The only thing that was different was we saw more deaders, which we expected considering I told him there had been infected in the area before.

Infected turn the dead.

Made sense.

The scenic route along the lake that Lev, me, and the kids had taken previously wasn't so scenic.

Again, it didn't surprise me.

We saw more bodies. Bodies of those who'd been violently ripped to shreds. Birds and animals picked at the carcasses. One particular body was covered with birds.

Fleck slowed down. "There you have it." He pointed.

"What?" I asked.

"That is why this will never end. We'll come to an end; it will look like it's over. You know, with only the dead ones left and us waiting for them to decay off. Then it will start again. No one will be able to figure out why, and that is why. Right there." He referenced the birds eating their dinner.

"You think?"

"Yeah, absolutely. Think about it," he said. "Bird flu."

"Bird flu?"

"I know it wasn't the bird flu, but birds can carry a flu, why not this?"

36

"I'm...pretty sure they mean chickens."

"No, all birds."

"No, I think just chickens."

"I miss fried chicken."

Silently I exhaled and bit my bottom lip in thought, watching as we rolled by. "Winter," I said. "Winter should kill them off."

"Maybe the infected. The dead are already dead. Ben and I discussed this."

"Really? What does Ben think?'

"He thinks it will freeze them, but they'll defrost and revive."

"I totally disagree."

"We'll find out, won't we?" Fleck tapped his hand on the steering wheel in a second of silence, then, "Fried rice. Not the type you get in Chinese restaurants, but like Hibachi."

I wanted to groan, I thought we had completed the food conversation and wandered what visual made him think of fried rice.

He was obsessed, reciting off what I believed was an entire Chinese take-out menu. Maybe that was Fleck's way of ignoring what was going on, or maybe he just thought it was good conversation.

We made it across the Thousand Islands Bridge, and of course Fleck had to bring up salad when we did that. He kept going back to the fried rice, adding, "What about yum yum sauce, come on you have to like yum yum sauce."

I made the mistake of mentioning I worked at Arby's before the world ended and that started an entire conversation. One that ended abruptly when we reached the road that led to the border.

The cars were still there, abandoned.

There had been a yellow Volkswagen, I remembered it, and it was still parked on the side of the road.

"This is it?" Fleck asked.

"Yeah this is it."

"Should we drive up to the border?"

"The helicopter will end up telling us to park and walk."

Fleck peered closer to the windshield. "I don't see a chopper."

"You will."

I felt it, something in my bones; it was different. It didn't look visually different, but it definitely was.

I think Fleck felt something too because he kept peering to the sky. "Are you sure it was like this when you were here before?" he asked.

"Positive. Pull over but leave the car where we can easily get to it."

Fleck did, parking carefully so no one would block us in.

I stepped out of the car and looked back to see Fleck grabbing the rifles. "They won't allow us to bring them in."

"Until I know for sure we aren't running into trouble, these come with us." He handed me one.

I placed the strap over my shoulder.

"How far is it?" he asked.

"Just up a ways. Maybe a quarter of a mile. As soon as we clear this crest we'll probably see people walking. Then when we hit the border, there will be people everywhere. It's buzzing. The camp that's beyond the fence is big and bright and full of life. It's just too bad it wasn't for us."

"Maybe there's a bigger reason."

I turned to walk backwards looking around.

"What is it?"

How to answer that; what to tell him? It wasn't the same. For as much as I wanted it to be, it wasn't. Something was off. It caused almost a feeling of dread in me. It felt empty. It was as if I could feel the silence.

"It's really quiet."

"Wasn't it before?"

"I guess. I don't know. I don't remember because we heard the chopper as soon as we got here."

"You would think we'd hear it."

"You would think. It's just…" I stopped walking and talking when we reached the crest. Unlike before there were no people making their way to the border.

It was an empty road. Not only was the roadway void of people, there was also a faint sound.

A creaking, like squeaky metal.

"Maybe everyone who was crossing already crossed," he said. "Nila?"

I faced him. "Something isn't right."

"Oh, you think? I have been questioning this since we pulled up and you decide now, right this second something is wrong."

"No, I said something isn't right."

"Same difference."

"No, it's not."

"Well, what do you want to do?" Fleck asked. "Keep going forward or go back?"

"Keep going."

Fleck pulled his rifle forward, and I did the same.

The creaking sound grew louder with each step we took until we were close enough to see the source.

"Keep going forward or go back?" Fleck repeated the question.

I didn't answer.

"I'm assuming it wasn't like this a couple weeks ago?"

He was being facetious. I glanced over at him then back to the border.

There were no guards, no people; the culprit of the noise was the gate. It had broken off its hinges and clanked against the frame with each slight breeze.

We were close enough to see something was wrong, but still too far away to know exactly what had happened. The main body of the camp was just a bit further across the border and through the fenced-in area.

"This border isn't secure," Fleck commented.

"Okay, stop," I told him. "This isn't a joke."

"I'm not joking. It's wide open, Nila. I don't see any…infected." He sniffed. "Or smell them, there's a good breeze, we should at least smell them."

He had a point; we could always smell them.

Did they get attacked or simply pull back? Surely, if they'd pulled back they'd have made sure the border was tight.

"Do you think it's safe?" I asked.

"I don't know."

We approached the gate. Fleck slung his rifle on his shoulder and tried to adjust the gate. It scraped loudly against the pavement, making enough noise to draw the dead forward.

We waited, making noise again, before deciding to step in.

Papers were scattered on the ground, the sign with the camp rules lay there with what looked like a smear of blood on the corner.

I reached out and pulled Fleck back, pointing down to the blood.

"Whatever was here," Fleck said, "is gone. It's too quiet."

There were two distinctive smells I had come to know when it came to death. The smell of a dead body and the smell of the dead.

The stench that hit us as we entered the camp wasn't the latter.

The sprawled-out refugee center, once filled with life, running children and white tents, had been desecrated.

Tents were torn, some burned. Bodies were everywhere.

My hand shot to cover my nose and mouth. Some of the bodies had been attacked, viciously and violently. There were bodies of infected as well, that was evident by the faces.

There was one thing they all had in common: they all had a bullet to the head. Even those who had died from being ripped apart.

"They didn't get attacked and lost," Fleck said. "This reminds me of the early days of the outbreak. When we fought back. When the soldiers took control."

"You think they pulled back?"

"It's hard to say, let's see what we can find." He took a step toward a tent.

"Stop," I told him.

"What? What's wrong?"

"Not that one," I said softly. I didn't need to verbally say it was the tent that we were in when Corbin was shot and Lev beaten, I think Fleck knew. He moved beyond it to a bigger tent.

"This one?" he asked.

I nodded. "That's the main check-in tent."

He parted the flap with his rifle, peeked inside and then walked in.

I followed.

When I had been in there before, the tent consisted of several check-in tables, then at the back was where they handed you the starter package: clothing, food, toiletries.

The tent appeared to have been cleared in a rush. Not everything had been taken—papers lay sprawled across the floor by the check-in tables creating a carpet of litter.

Fleck lifted a toppled table then bent down to pick up a clip-board. "Names," he said. "Looks like people they registered."

"How far back does it go?" I asked.

"This list...a few days." He set it down, then bent down to the floor. He began gathering the sheets of paper that were there. "Jesus, look at all these."

I shouldered my rifle and bent down to help him, glancing at the papers.

Mary Davidson, Erie Pennsylvania, fifty-seven

Matthew Diolus, Watertown NY, thirty-two.

Jennifer Marshman, Huntingdon Pennsylvania, thirty-eight

The list went on, at least twenty-five people on each sheet of paper, and there were hundreds of sheets left behind. I couldn't imagine how many sheets they took. Each listed a name and where they were from. But there was not one mention of *where they all went,* only if they had been transferred before the attack.

"They had it together," Fleck said. "Apparently."

"The big mistake was opening the borders."

"Wouldn't have mattered. This is just a checkpoint. I highly doubt they had guards posted at every border. Anyone could have gotten in. They tried to help. They tried to stay alive."

"Maybe it was just here."

"Could be." Fleck shrugged. "But if the infection made its way into Canada. It won't be long before it goes down. It's a matter of time." He set down his papers and walked across the tent.

I continued to lift the papers and collect them.

"What are you doing?" he asked.

"Taking these. I want to look through and see if I knew anyone. A lot of these people are from Erie, maybe Ben knows them. There are also a lot of sheets. I want to look for Sawyer and Billy. I know it's a longshot, but I want to see their names. See if they were transferred out before things went south here."

"I doubt they'll be on there."

"I know."

"But…I do want to look for them. I think as hard as it is going to be, we need to look."

I furrowed my brow. "What do you mean?"

"We need to check this camp," Fleck said. "There are a lot of bodies out there. We need to look. At least if we don't see them, we know they stood a chance of surviving this. You said they were protective over the kids, right? Hopefully when things got bad here they moved them out."

"Hopefully." I set down the papers. "I'll come back for these. Let's do this."

Fleck turned to leave the tent but stopped. I watched him bend down. "Well, I'll be damned."

"What is it?"

He lifted a brown package. "Meals Ready to Eat. Fried rice."

Slowly, I shook my head as he placed it on a table.

We began our task. The camp was huge, but we checked and looked at every single body, every single face. It took hours. A task that would keep us from returning to the cabin that day. We'd have to find a place safe to camp for the night. It was daunting and sad, so many people. I could see it on Fleck's face that it was a painful reminder of what he'd gone through early on. An experience Lev, myself and my daughter were spared.

On the positive side they saved more people than were killed. On the negative we didn't find Sawyer or Billy. I had to accept the reality that we probably never would find out what happened to them.

SEVEN

DIG IN

September 8

I could only imagine how upset and worried everyone had been when our radio call failed to make it through the previous day. We had tried every chance we got, but with no luck. Finally, we got through about twenty miles outside of Erie when we were almost home. They didn't sound relieved.

Well, Lev didn't. Ben took the radio from him to calmly tell us that he was glad we were fine—they were a little worried. Of course, Lev was in the background clarifying it was more than just a little.

Hal had radioed while we were gone. He had narrowly got out of Canada. They were where we had been three months earlier.

A warning, a little too late.

It didn't surprise me Lev was upset; it did shock me to see him walking out of the cabin the second we pulled up.

"What?" Fleck asked. "He is miraculously healed?"

"I doubt that. He's just stubborn." I got out of the car, and my daughter blasted by Lev on the porch and ran directly to me.

"Mommy! Lev had us worried."

She hugged my legs, and I lifted her to give her an embrace before setting her back down. My stare never left Lev. "I'm fine, sweetie."

"Did you find Sawyer?" she asked.

"No, baby, we didn't."

"I didn't think you would. Lev said it would be hard."

"What?" Lev nearly blasted. "I said no such thing. You asked how big Canada was and I said big. Your daughter draws her own conclusions."

"So she is mistaken when she said you had her worried?"

Ben interjected. "Nope, she's right on that one. He had us all a nervous wreck. He was very tense."

"I was worried," Lev said.

"The head injury doesn't help," added Ben. "Things tend to be a bit more emotional when you have a head injury."

"Lev, you should be resting," I told him.

"Nila, I have been resting for two weeks. I think I've had enough rest."

"So Canada was bad?" Ben asked.

Before answering, I told Katie to go back inside the cabin. "It looked as if they were attacked," I told him. "The soldiers fought back, and it looked like they just packed up and moved out."

"In a hurry," Fleck added as he approached the porch. "There were too many dead to count. I don't know if the infected came from within or hit the camp. We don't know if it's only the borders or all over. I was telling Nila, it looked like it did in the beginning for us. You remember, an area would be hit, they'd kill all the sick and evacuate everyone else."

I glanced at Lev. "We missed that."

"What now?" Ben asked.

Lev answered, "We wait. There's no reason to leave this cabin. We have all we need, fresh water and a means to stay warm."

"I agree," I said. "Winter is coming—not in the, like, *Game of Thrones* way. Maybe it would be, with all the undead. Anyhow..." I waved out my hand. "I think winter will kill them off. I think it'll be over after a good freeze. We can figure out what's next after that. Until then, we get supplies for the baby, anything else we need, start gathering wood, and dig in."

EIGHT

BUZZED

November 14

There is a lot to miss when the world comes to a screeching halt. For people like Fleck it was fast food and takeout, for others it was the internet and television. Those, though, are easily remedied or a substitution can be found.

We used the solar generator to power the television and not only did we have hundreds of DVDs, my father had stashed old VHS tapes as well.

Fleck found his solution to takeout. Or rather pizza. One day he just up and left, telling us he had a run he needed to do and wanted to do it alone.

No one condoned him going alone, but there was no arguing with Fleck. He took a trip to Dayton to a survival food warehouse. Not only did he find more of his dehydrated, Chinese survival food, he found survival food pizza kits. The cheese wasn't real, but it worked. It was awesome.

I think my biggest 'miss' was knowing what the weather was going to be.

I missed having a weather forecast.

I made the mistake of telling this to Lev and he immediately started tossing out stuff to me.

Red sky at night, sailor's delight...

Count the chirps of a cricket for fourteen seconds and add forty...

Winds from the south bring rain in the mouth...

"What the hell, Lev?"

"Without relying on the app or television, your body will tell you what the weather will be," he said.

He had told me that just after we really started digging in and I didn't believe him at first.

Then I got it.

We made constant supply runs. Lev had finally recovered by the end of September and had started to alternate with us.

There wasn't much we didn't get. We got everything from food and toys to winter clothing.

Then I could sense the weather was changing.

The shed was packed.

We would hold meetings to think of things we would need.

Ben and I had just gotten back from what I believed would be the last supply run for a while. Everyone helped unload. The entire floorboard storage was packed, as was the shed. We had to play a cleaver game of Tetris with the items to make them fit, and still boxes and supplies lined the walls of every room of the cabin.

We were like hoarders.

But we had enough, at least until there was a break in the snow, whenever that came.

It was going to be hard to predict what the roads would be like after a snowstorm. Without maintenance, would they even be passable? It wasn't going to be long until the snow would come.

Once again, Lev was right: I felt it. I didn't need Bill Montana, the weatherman from the dedicated weather channel, to tell me. And my bones were certainly better than the local station WPXI.

After Lev had told me to get over missing the weather channel, I had become quite good at predicting what was going to happen. I even had better accuracy tuning into the subtle pings and pain signals my body gave.

In fact, I marked down my predictions and what the actual weather ended up being.

But I knew it was coming.

Snow.

After dinner, and watching Katie work on her drawings, I went outside to enjoy the porch before the cold and snow would make it impossible. I also wanted to enjoy the quiet. Christian was fussy and crying every fifteen minutes.

I put a blanket on the top porch step to sit on. I had a bottle of expensive bourbon I'd grabbed on a run, so I poured some into a mug then lit a cigarette.

It was only a minute or two before I heard the screen porch open. I honestly thought it was going to be Katie until I heard the uneven thump from Lev's limp.

Ben had finally given the go ahead to take the cast off. His head-aches had taken months to subside, and he was putting some of the weight back on. Those high-calorie Meals Ready to Eat helped and he was using the chopping of wood as his own exercise routine.

We ended up with a lot of wood. So much so that it made a second barrier to our fence.

"Aw, Nila," he said with a scolding whine. "You're smoking again."

"Yeah, I am."

"But if you're going to hold the baby…"

I just looked at him.

"That's right, you don't like holding babies."

"Correction, I don't like babies. Not until they're mobile. Christian isn't bad. He just has his fussy nights. I'll help when I can, I'm just the last resort."

49

"Yes, we know."

I patted the spot next to me. "Did you bring a glass?"

"I knew you were out here, so yes." Lev sat down. "I saw that stash you picked up."

"Thinking I may need to be Lisa two. You know, my stepmother."

"She was funny. She would put that straw in the small bottle of Jack and it was like her own personal juice box."

"I know, and she never got drunk." I poured some booze into Lev's cup. "I never got that."

"She was a professional."

"She was." I smiled.

"That's nice to see." Lev reached out touching my cheek with his index finger. "A smile."

"They happen."

"Not when we talk about those we lost."

"That's gonna be a little harder. One day at a time." I hit my cigarette and sipped my drink.

"So, are you waiting on the snow?" Lev asked

I glanced at him curiously. "Why would you say that?"

"You're sitting out here. It doesn't look like you came out here for a break. You're out here for a while. The blanket, the booze, the smokes. You're waiting on the snow."

"I am. It's gonna happen. The sky is dark. I can't see the stars or moon. And it's quiet. It's always so quiet before it snows."

"It's a dead world, Nila, it's quiet all the time."

"That's true," I said.

"And your feet hurt?"

"Did I tell you that?" I asked,

"When we were thirteen. You used to tell me the soles of your feet would hurt right before it started to snow. That's why I said you don't need a weatherman."

"It's impressive that you remember that," I said.

"I also remember all the times you would sit on your father's porch, like this, waiting for the first snow."

"That's because I was always hoping it would snow a ton so we didn't have school. Then when I got older I dreaded the thought of it. Now...it's okay. I just wish my father was here to yell at me or Katie for causing condensation on the windows while watching the snow. Or seeing my brother, Bobby, who would just run straight out the cabin door and belly flop into it."

"I used to love when we got snowed in up here," Lev said. "And Big Bears Campground annual sled off."

"Days," I said, crinkling my nose. "Days we would get stuck."

"See there is much more to miss than a weatherman."

"Yeah, there is. The biggest is my daughter Addy." I inhaled sharply taking a moment. "Now there...there's a person who...it's gonna be a long time before I talk about her..." I felt my throat swell and the words choked me. "Think..." I cleared my throat. "Before I think about her and smile. It's so difficult." I sniffed hard and finished my drink, pouring some more.

"It will come. The day will come."

"Promise?" I said with a breaking voice.

"I promise."

I downed another drink.

"Wow, you are practicing to be Lisa."

"Comfortably numb. Just doing a lot of thinking today. Some days it hits me. So I thought I'd drink a little and wait for the snow."

"We have nowhere to go."

"Not yet."

51

Lev stared out. "I wish all of you would just get that thought out of your minds. Everyone wants to go somewhere. Go where? We have all that we need here, we can make this work."

"I think we need to see what's out there."

"We have. So unless everyone plans on going west or really south, there's not much more to see," Lev said. "The only problem with going so far away is we'll just turn around and come back here."

"You think?" I asked.

Lev nodded.

"I bet that doesn't happen."

"I'll take that bet," Lev said extending his hand.

I shook it.

"Your hands are cold," Lev said.

"Oh, I have gloves." I tossed my cigarette and pulled my gloves from my coat pockets. "I forgot."

"I see you have a new winter coat."

"Yes, I do. I didn't bring one. Obviously it was almost summer when we got here. I grabbed three today. This one will be good when we go hunting next week for turkeys."

Lev chuckled. "Nila, it's thin. Very thin. It's cold now, you must be freezing."

"No, I'm good. Honestly...feel." I held out my arm.

Lev touched my coat. "Why does this coat feel hot?"

"It's a heated jacket. Battery in the back. It's freaking awesome. I picked it up at the sporting goods store."

"That's almost like cheating the winter."

"Yeah, it is," I said with a partial smile. "You know, when Ben and I were out today we didn't see any of them. None. Well, none walking."

"We didn't see any yesterday either."

"The ones we saw the other day, they were so slow, some were falling apart." I shook my head. "I wasn't even a little scared. They weren't a threat."

"Don't underestimate them," Lev said. "Remember how Cade got bit? One of them on the floor of the pharmacy."

"That's true. But the fast ones, the really mobile ones, they're gone." I looked at him. "Do you think it's over?"

"What do you mean?"

"I mean. Maybe we became the new Canada and we're infection free. Everyone who got it is gone. What do you think?"

"I think we can hope. I would like to believe so. But truthfully, it's probably only a pause, because as long as this virus is out there in some way, shape, or form…" Lev said. "It will never be over."

THE NOW

NINE

SOMEWHERE ELSE TO BE

May 1

Where were they?

The days of winter drew to an end, and I even believed that Lev was ready to leave.

It didn't take long for us to discover what cabin fever was truly like.

We'd secured what supplies we could in the floorboard storage. By the first of April, with no direction but south, we had packed up the station wagon and along with Fleck on the motorcycle, we left the cabin.

I did so with every intention of going back, not because I wanted to, but because I didn't want to feel defeated if things didn't turn out. In my mind I could always justify it as I never meant to stay away from the cabin anyhow.

The wagon was crowded, but we didn't want to chance depending on a second full-size vehicle only to not be able to fuel it up.

So we stopped…a lot. With two children, one of which was nearly a year old, we had to.

Many times it was overnight. We were in no rush. But still, not once did we run into an infected or deader.

We also didn't run into many people. A person here or there. Twice we ran into a small group. We didn't interact much or stay with them. We just exchanged information and knowledge. One of the groups had been to Canada and left just as the virus broke out there. They told us they were searching for something called The Colony. They'd heard about it when they were in Canada. It was supposed to be a city in the US that had restructured and rebuilt. Things were normal there or at least the way normal used to be.

The other group had no intention of leaving the place they called home. A small trailer park in West Virginia where they had started their own farm. There were twelve people.

Of course, Lev liked them and said they had the right idea.

I believe the lack of seeing infected or many people was because we never once went near a major city and avoided major roadways at all cost.

Still, I placed in my mind that it was over. The outbreak, the dead…over. It had been a year. My God, an entire year had passed since a huge part of my life had been taken away. While the hole still remained in my heart and soul, it was time to move on, to rebuild.

Maybe we could find The Colony, or whatever it was.

We did, however, find a man named Westin Hiller. He was our gold mine.

He was sitting outside of the Cobb Corner Police Station as we passed through the one stoplight town of Cobb Corner in the southernmost part of Virginia. The sign just before town boasted a population of six hundred and three. Somehow that was probably inaccurate.

Westin was an older gentleman, but stout and strong looking. He wore a pair of blue jeans, a clean T-shirt, sunglasses and sat with his rifle perched across his lap.

He waved from his chair. Not flagging us. Just waving as if we were tourists passing through.

Fleck was in the lead and stopped first, then we did.

His introduction to us was a, "Holy Cannoli, look at you folks piling out of that wagon."

And in the first few minutes of meeting him we learned he had been the chief of police at one point, before everything went to hell, and there were fourteen people still living in the sprawled-out community.

We also learned the big strong man hadn't lost his humanity or heart as he facially crumbled, eyes glossing over when he saw Christian. He asked to hold him, then cradled him like a child he hadn't seen in a long time. I didn't need to ask why he reacted that way. It was obvious.

It was also obvious that our next place to spend the night was going to be right there in Westin's town.

He told us we were welcome to stay as long as we wanted, and that everyone did their part to keep the town going.

The kids were tired from traveling, and Bella took them to the tiny park. Fleck took guard, even though Westin assured us there were no Ragers and hadn't been any for months.

"Even in a small town like Cobb," Westin said. "We seen it. We lost a lot early on because people were trying to go somewhere, anywhere, and would take the secondary highways, like you folks. I should have shut us down." He shook his head. "We tried to help."

"I'm a doctor," Ben said. "I don't know if you have one, but I would be happy to help while I'm here if someone needs it."

Weston's eyes lit up. "You're really a doctor?"

Ben nodded. "I am."

"Well, we have about three people who will be happy to hear that. We've been at a loss. Bryers has a nasty cough he just can't shake. There's a bigger pharmacy in the next town. I can take you."

"Well let's see what I need first," Ben said.

I loved Ben. He was such a kind and gentle man. Every time he did something good or acted kind, I saw where Cade had gotten it from.

With a wave of his hand, Westin took us to the station. "Gonna radio them to get them closer. They can make it to you for treatment," he said.

He led us up a flight of stairs, then to what I thought was the mayor's office because of the name on the door. Then we walked in.

More than likely because it was the best room in the house and on the second floor, Westin and his people had transformed it into some sort of radio room. There was one main radio, a big one and a bunch of smaller ones. A huge map of the United States hung on the wall. It was so huge it looked like wallpaper.

A younger man sat in a swivel chair and turned when we walked in.

"Carl, these folks are with that motorcycle you heard coming," Westin said. "This is Nila and Ben. He's a doctor."

Carl shook our hands.

"I wanna get the word out that we have a doctor here if anyone needs him. And this is..." Westin snapped his finger and pointed at Lev. "Didn't get your name."

"Lev," he answered.

"Lev?" Westin asked. "What's that short for?"

"Levon."

"Spelled like the song."

"Yes."

"Man of few words."

I laughed. "Sorry. No, he's not. Just around new people. Don't get him started."

Lev cast a glare my way. I turned my head and really looked at the map. There were markings all over it. Red and blue, and occasionally black Xs.

"What is this?" I asked. "What are the areas that are marked?"

"Life. People that passed through and people we communicate with. The Xs are areas that were once alive but now…they're gone," Weston replied.

Lev walked to the map. "Presley, West Virginia. We ran into people that are settled there."

"Excellent." Weston lifted a marker and gave it to Lev. "Just color it in."

"Have you heard of something called The Colony?" I asked.

"You know…people have asked and I don't know what to tell them. I know what it's supposed to be," Westin said. "But no place called The Colony has reached out to us. We're on the radio a lot. I was wondering if they meant Key West. But it's not a major city. The Colony is supposed to be some major city the military went into about nine months ago, cleaned house, and started securing it and walling it in."

Ben whistled. "Can't be that big of a major city. Wall it all in? Cordoning it off would take a lot of effort."

"Unless," Lev said, "it's a 'back against the wall' type. Like on a lake—that would mean one whole side is already taken care of. Or a river."

"Pittsburgh," Westin said. "That would be easy to do. Cut off the bridges and you only need one wall. Straight across, through the city river to river."

"Wouldn't that be funny for us," I commented. "Considering we're from there. And headed to the mountains."

"We bypassed it on the way south," Lev said. "All the major cities."

"Probably why no one could see it," Westin said.

"Well, how are they filling it?" Ben asked. "If no one can find it or knows where it is?'

"Maybe you don't find it," Westin replied. "Maybe they find you."

"That would have to be the way it is," Lev said. "They're not broadcasting. We did hear Florida has parts that are good."

"They do," Westin replied. "Some more cautious than others about who travels there. You have places where people kinda just stopped and settled. No real community. Then you have places like Key West that has law and order."

"The Keys?" I asked.

Westin nodded. "They were hit pretty bad. They shut down the road once they got it under control. Now they'll let you in, but they have a vigorous check-in system to make sure no one brings it back. Then again, Canada did too. How it got it, I don't know."

I looked at Lev.

Westin must have noticed the expression on my face. "What?"

"Keys are out for us," I said. "We went to Canada."

"I was pretty adamant they should go," said Ben. "One of our group had been bit early on in the outbreak, got sick, but never turned. I thought for sure he'd be a shot at a cure."

"They killed him," I said. "Right in front of his kid. No hesitation. They just shot him. And…and…" I glanced again at Lev. "My daughter was bit as well last year. She didn't get sick and didn't turn. They almost killed her, too, had Lev not jumped in."

"I'm sorry to hear that," Westin said. "I heard Canada was really stringent. I heard about the execution laws."

"You kind of understand them," I said. "Until it happens to you. So the Keys are out for us."

"Maybe not. Carl, get them on the radio," Westin instructed. "Let's find out."

Carl put out the radio call, and a few minutes later spoke to a woman named Gloria. She told him if the bite mark was healed and scarred over, there wouldn't be an issue. And even if there was, they certainly didn't have the execution rules.

I was relieved to hear that but was still uncertain.

62

"Do you have a destination?" Westin asked.

Lev shook his head. "We're looking. Hell, we don't even have a list of what qualifies as a good place. I guess we'll know when we find it."

"Fresh water and safety would be one," Westin said. "Whatever you're searching for, I hope you find it. Because you need to find a place and stop."

"Isn't movement life?" I asked.

"No." Westin shook his head. "At least I didn't think so. When you settle, you take root. Roots mean growth, growth is life. At least that's what I think."

Lev gave me an 'I told you so' glance. He remembered our arguments about movement being life.

"You know there's a place that's not bad. Marco Island." Westin walked to the map and pointed to it. "It's easily accessible. There's people there. You may not see them because they're scattered about, but we radio them often. And if you change your mind, you can always head to the Keys because Key West is taking people in all the time. Heck, if you can boat, boat there. They have checkpoints at their piers."

"I can boat," Ben said. "Been a boater all my life."

It actually sounded like a semi plan.

Westin showed us around town while Ben examined half the residents that showed up at the police station with questions about their health.

Cobb Corner was a good stop. A good place, and much to Lev's dismay we only stayed a week, promising that we'd stay in touch.

I did however, go to the back of the wagon and retrieve the registration list of names I had found in Canada. I figured since Westin was in contact with so many people, he'd be the best one to have that list.

Staying in contact was the way Westin was able to keep information flowing and a way to know the world was still going.

And by the looks of the map, even if it was a minuscule fraction of what it used to be, the world was still surviving.

TEN

SETTLED

May 9

Westin stayed with us. Not in the physical sense, but we learned a lot from him.

He and Cobb Corner were vital in the decision and direction we took. We got to know each and every one of them during our stay. They made us feel at home, and when we left they gave us food packs and juice.

Fleck was probably the biggest proponent for going all the way to Florida. The whole trip was bringing back memories for him of after the original outbreak. Fleck and his group had migrated north and now he was returning home. When Westin mentioned the place where there were people, Fleck's eyes lit up.

"My grandparents lived in Naples," he said. "I know the place well."

It was settled. It was a destination.

We couldn't get to the actual island part with the nifty ports and resorts. There had been a lot of flooding there, at least that's what we were told. Our welcoming committee was a man in a flowered shirt, holding a case of beer and walking from the beer distributor.

"Coming, going, or passing through?" he asked as he approached our car.

"Not passing through," Lev answered. "Actually, we want to ground ourselves for a while. Westin from Cobb told us about this place."

"Aw, good old Westin. The ears of the world. Well if he sent you, he probably radioed."

"I believe he did. He mentioned Marco Island."

"You're in Marco city. The island was flooded last week and is still dangerous to get to."

"Is there someone in charge of your group?" Lev asked.

"Um, not really," he answered. "People kind of do their own thing. Except our radio woman. She lives at the Wave RV resort. Why, what's up?"

"We just wanted to get situated somewhere. He"—Lev pointed to Fleck—"has family in the area. He wanted to go to their home."

"I see. Well, a lot of people left. About seventy-five percent of the boats left the port. They may have gone."

"They're elderly."

The guy shrugged. "Still. Old don't mean dead now does it."

I leaned over Lev. "Speaking of dead, have there been any lately?"

"Not around here. I haven't seen them since winter. It's as if they migrated like birds."

"Are there campgrounds around here anywhere?" Lev asked.

There Lev went, gravitating to a campground. His comfort zone, I suppose.

"Actually, there's a KOA RV campground with cabins about seven miles from here," he said. "A few people settled there. The whole place isn't cleaned up. You'll have to clear your own spot, but that's a good starting place. Less mayhem there when the shit hit."

"We appreciate it." Lev got out of the car and walked to Fleck. I could see them speaking but couldn't hear what they were saying.

66

It had something to do with a campsite, I was sure of it. When Lev returned we followed Fleck.

"We never got his name," I said to Fleck.

"No, we didn't."

"It was a little rude of us," Ben said. "At least we thanked him. That was a good thing."

"So was not getting his name," Bella said.

I turned to the back seat when she said that. "What do you mean?"

Bella shrugged, talking as she looked down to the baby. "Not because we don't want to know names or get close because people were dying, but because it means the world is going back to normal. We're going back to not caring who a person is."

I watched as Katie poked Bella's arm and whispered, "I don't think she really cared before."

My eyes widened and I spun back around in my seat.

Lev looked at me with a twitch of his head. "She's your daughter."

Fleck was a pretty strong man emotionally. But at times I thought maybe it was his way of handling things—convince others he is strong to cover any weakness that stirred inside. Been there, done that, I am that.

Although I knew I was finally on my way to healing, Fleck was about to face something that could set him back.

His grandparents' home.

He was with me when I returned to my own home and my father's house, so I wanted to be there for him.

I remembered the feeling of walking into my old home, the way the memories of a good life came flooding back. How I ached and longed for one more dinner around our kitchen table. One more end of the month worrying about how we were going to pay bills because I had quit another job or had taken days off. Robbing Peter to pay Paul so we had enough available credit for Christmas.

Life wasn't easy at times. We weren't rich, far from it, but life was good.

It was different going to Fleck's grandparents' home. He told me that. They had only bought it ten years earlier, and his grandmother lived there, often alone, until his grandfather had retired.

It wasn't the memories of a childhood home he sought but the essence of a grandparent's love.

Unlike when we had rolled onto my street, it looked like there had been very little chaos in the gated, senior living community.

I expected bungalows. What we saw were beautiful homes with gardens and lawns that had, at one time, been well maintained. There was no litter in the streets. No strange FEMA markings on the doors, no bodies.

We pulled up to his grandparents' home. The drapes were closed and there wasn't a car in the carport. That didn't mean anything though—someone else could have taken the car. We had done so.

The house was a cute one-story home. We checked all the doors only to find they were locked. No hidden keys like in the movies. Fleck had to break in through the kitchen door. I stood ready with my weapon.

Once we got the back door open, we made more noise and waited.

Nothing.

No infected came for us.

There was a musty humid smell to the house, but there was no smell of death. No blood, no signs of sickness or a struggle.

The kitchen was impeccably in order. Unlike my own home which had been turned into a mess in our desperation to leave.

"It's so neat in here," I said.

"I wouldn't be surprised if my grandmother was like"—Fleck proceeded to do what I thought was a Jewish grandmother imitation—"oh, it's the end of the world, I have to make sure the house is clean. I don't want people coming in here and saying that I lived in filth."

I giggled and turned to the fridge. It was speckled with perfect flower refrigerator magnets. One held a business card for air-conditioning repairs, another a doctor appointment reminder.

There was a photo. A family picture taken on a boat. Fleck was in it. He had to be about fifteen or sixteen. He stood between what I guessed were his parents and grandparents. They looked so happy.

"Is this your dad?" I asked, pointing to the dark-haired man.

"Yeah, it is."

"Wow, you look just like him. And your grandparents." I referenced the older couple that looked as if they were in a commercial. Perfect sailing clothes with bright smiles. "They look very, how can I put it...proper."

Fleck laughed. "They weren't. They just looked the part. My grandfather was a professor. He taught engineering. Really smart guy. Smart enough to build a bridge. But smart enough to survive the apocalypse? I don't know."

"He looks like he knows what to do. Hey...Fleck is this you?" I lifted the school picture of a smiling, toothless little boy with a crew cut.

"Yeah, second grade."

"Oh my God. How precious." I placed it in my pocket.

"What are you doing?"

"One day you'll thank me for taking that."

I watched as he took an obviously nervous breath. "I'm going to go check the bedroom and see if they're…"

"Yeah, go on."

I figured while he did that, I'd look for more memorabilia for Fleck to take. Men tended not to think like that. I walked to the living room. There was a huge fireplace. As a person from the north, the fireplace didn't make sense being in a Florida house. A painting of a little girl hung over an oddly empty mantel.

I looked everywhere in the living room and dining room. There were no pictures. Only the ones on the fridge.

There was no noise coming from the bedrooms, and I took that as a good sign. I really didn't think Fleck would find his grandparents in the house. I returned to the kitchen and opened the first cabinet…glasses. The second…dishes. The next…empty.

It was empty? Nothing was in there. Certainly, if salvagers had come, they were the neatest salvagers I had seen. The contents of the fourth cabinet surprised me.

Perched on the lower shelf was a single bowl. In it a can of soup, a small package of crackers and a bottle of apple juice. Almost as if it had been deliberately left there for someone coming and looking for food.

I heard the scuffling of footsteps approaching and I turned. "Fleck, I…"

"Nothing," he said. "No bodies."

"They're not here," I said and pointed to the cabinet. "They packed up and left. Took everything but left this in case someone came to find food."

"Holy shit."

"Looks to me like your grandparents survived the outbreak."

Fleck agreed. We searched the house for more evidence they'd left. Although we wouldn't know clothing items that were missing.

There wasn't any medication in the house at all. Not even an aspirin. We were certain of our conclusion.

At the time of the outbreak, they were smart, thinking ahead...and most importantly, alive.

<><><><>

By the time Fleck and I returned, Lev and Ben had our new place nearly ready. The campground wasn't bad. Not much to clean up. About three quarters of the RV spots were empty. I half expected us to be in one big RV. Instead, they had lay claim to the four cabins in the center area near the office. They were really cute: all white with white square pillars that graced the porches and small patches of grass around them. The center common area between them was a masonry patio with a fire pit surrounded by neatly set up lawn chairs.

I complimented them on a job well done and gave a smug comment to Lev about how it was decked out compared to Big Bear.

"Yes, well." Lev pointed to the small fenced-in pool area a hundred feet away. "At least the Big Bear pool was set away from everything.'

"True."

"Are these the only cabins?" I asked.

"No," Ben said. "There are groups of small ones on the south end in a really nice secluded area. By the river, too, for fishing."

"Not saying this isn't great, but...why didn't we use those?"

"Taken," Lev replied. "There's a large group of people down there. We introduced ourselves and got their names." He winked.

"Wow, and they weren't protective about strangers moving in? They were okay?"

Lev looked at Ben before answering.

"Ah, Lev, tell me you didn't kill them," I said.

"What? No. Nila, you of all people." He shook his head. "They weren't happy at first until I told them Ben was a doctor. He's already given someone stiches."

"Apparently, I'm gonna set up in the office," Ben said. "They already contacted the Marco radio lady about me."

"Hey, at least we're welcome now."

"And we have fish." Ben clapped his hands together. "Which I will cook for us tonight."

"I can cook," I said.

"No." Ben shook his head. "Just...no."

He did cook the meal, and we enjoyed it in the common area. The baby was quiet and went to bed early, so did Katie and Bella. I guess they were tired from traveling.

When Ben turned in, Fleck, Lev and I sat around a small fire. Which I thought was redundant because it was hot. I guess we needed light.

"This is a lot like the cabin," Lev said. "I feel comfortable here."

"It's like home," I said. "For the time being, right?"

"Nila, you need to think about this need to move. We were on the road for six weeks. I really want to stop for a while. Katie and Chris need to stop. Even Bella, she acts strong, but she's still a kid."

"I know." I sipped my drink. "I also know you would be happy going back to the cabin and never leaving."

"I didn't want to leave in the first place."

"Can I..." Fleck lifted his hand. "Can I say something?"

Lev and I gave him our attention.

"Lev, you talk all the time about never leaving the cabin. In my opinion, we did kind of need to leave," Fleck said. "It was nice. It was self-sufficient. But it was just the seven of us."

"And what's wrong with that?" Lev asked.

"Life has to go on, dude," Fleck said. "We need to interact with people. Meet people. Maybe even find someone. Someone who makes us want to keep going. I get that you don't get that. I mean, why would you. You guys have each other. You're a couple."

"We're not a couple," Lev said.

"Yeah, but you…" Fleck pointed to the cabin. "You have your little set up in there."

"But we're not a couple."

"Um…" I hummed out. "In a way…yeah, he's right, we're a couple."

"We are?"

"Yeah, if you look at it in a non-technical way," I said. "We're a couple, we just don't, you know…have sex."

"You don't?" Fleck asked.

"Nila," Lev nearly scolded.

"Just saying." I shrugged. "We're a couple in all ways but that way. We don't have sex. We probably will never have sex."

"You won't?" Fleck asked.

"Why…why are you saying this?" Lev stuttered his words.

"It's true." I looked at Fleck. "It's probably true…"

"Why wouldn't you sleep with him?" Fleck asked.

"Do we need to discuss this?" Lev questioned. "Because I don't really want to know."

I ignored Lev and answered Fleck. "We have known each other forever. We've been friends forever. I love Lev. And you know, if I wasn't his friend, yeah…he's hot. But…what if it's bad?"

"Dude."

I faced Lev, his mouth agape. "Lev, seriously, what if it's bad? Then things will never be the same with us. We'll both be like, uh, what can I say to get out of doing it again? I can't claim my period all

73

the time. Yeah, I can see it." I took a drink. "Both of us on our backs, lying in bed in that awkward after silence. You're thinking, I can't believe that happened. That's never happened to me before."

"Dude," Fleck laughed the word.

"I mean…" Before I could say anymore, Lev had stood and walked away.

"You did that to him on purpose, didn't you?" Fleck asked.

"Yeah, yeah, I did." I looked to our cabin and could see Lev moving about inside. Sitting back, I brought my drink to my lips. "I think I'm gonna like it here."

ELEVEN

FROM LEV'S SIDE

May 13

"I hate it here," Nila said to me.

I knew it though.

I knew it was coming. When I returned from getting supplies, she barreled out of our cabin toward me.

Here it comes, I thought.

I don't know where she got it from, but since the outbreak she had been so unsettled.

"Nila, it's only been four days."

"I know."

"It's nice here. It really is."

And it was. Those who lived in the southern part of the campgrounds called Meadow Area were nice. There was a little boy Katie's age that came to play with her. He was a larger boy, and I would look at them and think how much they reminded me of Nila and myself.

Other than the boy, they didn't really socialize with us, but would give us a morning fishing report.

Ben wanted to fish in the ocean and had already found a boat.

"Tell me what it is about this place that you don't like?" I asked her.

"Um for one…" She pointed to the cabin.

"You don't like the cabin? It is very nice."

"It's small, Lev. There's no real kitchen."

"I can build you a kitchen, Nila. Not that you'll use it."

"Hey now."

"Anything else?"

She pointed again to the cabin. "The porch. The top step." She walked over and sat on it. "You can't fit with me."

"We can sit on the patio."

"I don't want to sit on the patio, Lev, I like sitting on the steps of a porch."

"Then we'll build a bigger porch."

"You have an answer for everything."

"No, Nila, I don't," I said. "I just don't think your reasons are valid. Katie seems content. Everyone is weary from traveling. Do you want to look for somewhere else in this town?"

Nila sighed out. "It will all suck."

"Nila, I'm sorry you aren't happy. What can I do to help?"

"You can start by…" With an irritated tone she smacked her own arm. "Finding me some bug spray. Fucking mosquitos."

"We had mosquitos back home."

"Not this monstrous and not this—" Suddenly, she inhaled sharply and loudly.

"What?"

"Oh my God."

"What?" I repeated.

"Mosquitos."

"Okay."

"Lev. Lev." She grabbed my arms. "What if the virus is carried by mosquitos? Fleck thinks it could be birds that are causing the outbreak to keep going. But what about mosquitos? Think about it...Zika?"

Out of every outlandish thing Nila had ever said to me, this theory was so plausible it caused me to pause.

"See?" Nila asked.

Not wanting her to know that I did find validity in her concerns, because it would make her worse, I tried to play it off. "No, I don't see."

"Lev, I'd be a goner if that mosquito had just bit an infected."

"Then good thing for you we haven't seen any infected." I attempted to walk away, when I heard her subtle growl. "Nila, I am not combatting everything you say intentionally."

"Yes, you are."

"Alright, yes, I am. But I just want you to give it a chance here, okay? Give it more than a couple days. Please."

She stared up at me, then her head turned suddenly to the sound of a screen porch door hitting and Katie laughing and running.

"See, Katie is happy."

Nila nodded. "You're right. You're right. I promise to give it a chance. Who knows," she said less convincingly. "Who knows what will happen."

ELEVEN

GOES WITHOUT SAYING

May 24

The sand was warm, making its way between my toes. It felt good and was about the only positive thing I could think of at that moment. Not that I didn't love Florida, but that was when there was a world with take-out restaurants and air conditioning.

It was hot, too hot for my liking. We were northerners. While we were used to humidity, the extreme heat of May was a lot.

There were reminders that we, at least those of us on the mend, remembered the world wasn't always such a horrible place. Things like a baby's laugh. Every time I got lost in thought, deep and depressing, like an emotional alarm clock, Christian would cry or laugh. Reiterating, like it or not, life goes on.

Standing on the beach, a good distance from the water's edge, I looked over my shoulder to Bella. She sat on the sand, no towel, holding the baby's hands as he tried to stand. She moved his arm in a wave. "Say hi to Nila."

"You put sunscreen on him, right?" I asked. "Lev grabbed some from that hotel."

"Yes, he's lathered," Bella answered.

"And you?"

She just stared at me.

"Okay, Okay." I lifted my hand in a wave. The young woman had matured years in the short time I'd known her, and I was mothering her. It was a habit. I was what could be called a 'helicopter mom.' I turned to my right to look at Katie. She had wanted to go to the beach. I wouldn't let her near the water; however she was inching awfully close.

"Katie, back up!" I hollered. "You're too close."

From a distance I heard Fleck's voice as he yelled back, "She's fine." He had pulled the lifeguard chair back some and was sat there with the rifle perched across his lap.

"She's not fine, she's too close," I spoke loudly, then turned back to Katie. "Katie! Back up."

"She only has her feet in there."

"Well, I worry about the riptide."

"Christ, Nila. You have to be in the water for the riptide to get you, it doesn't have arms that reach out and grab you."

"She's in the water."

"Her toes only."

Not wanting to scream so he could hear me, I made my way closer.

I don't know how he did it. He was wearing jeans, a T-shirt and that bike bandana.

"Aren't you hot?" I asked.

"Yeah, I hate this shit," he answered.

"How are you gonna jump in and save someone if they drown?"

He peered down to me, then looked out to the ocean. "Who?"

"There are three of us here."

"Bella is way back there, you're here and Katie isn't even getting wet. Besides, I'm not getting in the water. Lev has me here in case of trouble. You can save whoever drowns."

"I don't swim," I replied.

"Then they all drown. Wait…" he said. "How did you spend every summer at that cabin and Big Bear without swimming?"

"I did swim, then Lev caused me to nearly drown and I instantly forgot how."

"I'll have to ask him about that," Fleck replied. "Speaking of which." He pointed to Lev.

My big friend was making his way toward us. He had buzzed his dark hair a little shorter, and he moved with a slight limp. I would never mention it though. Lev didn't believe he had a limp. He was convinced he was at a hundred percent, and who was I to tell him any different.

What I didn't understand was the need for him to wear not only jeans, but a long-sleeve shirt and work boots.

"Where's Ben?" I asked as Lev approached.

"He's cleaning fish. He had a good day."

"Did you go fishing with him?" I asked. "Probably not."

"No, I had other things. How is the day at the beach?"

"Boring. There isn't much to do. Aren't you hot?" I asked.

"Yes," Lev answered. "Very."

"Then why are you overdressed?"

"Because when night comes and it cools, I take off these clothes and feel much cooler."

"Oh stop, that doesn't work." I laughed.

"She has a point," Fleck added. "Plus, I would have thought you especially wouldn't be able to handle the heat."

"Why me especially?" Lev asked. "Because I am tall."

"No, because you were from Russia. It's always cold there. I would think it's in your blood," Fleck said.

"First of all, I am not Russian. Not even close. I was adopted from Serbia."

"Ah." Fleck nodded.

"Anyhow," Lev said. "I was at the—"

"Did you cause Nila to almost drown?" Fleck interrupted. "I'm sorry I wanted to ask before I forgot."

"What? No." Lev shook his head.

"Yes, you did, Lev, remember?" I asked. "Seventh grade you knocked me into the deep end of the Big Bear pool, I wasn't ready and nearly drowned."

"That wasn't me, it was Ricky Langston, and I was the one who pulled you out."

"Oh, that's right thanks."

"How do you not remember these things, Nila? Anyhow," he said, "I was at the home and hardware stores."

"Were they pretty much picked over?"

"No, not really. I was getting ideas for the cabin."

"Any of them have to do with power or AC?"

"No," he replied firmly. "I'll hook up the solar generator and you can use the little unit."

"I'll never leave that room. And it's hot everywhere."

"You'll get used to it."

"Oh, I doubt it. Lev…it's been two weeks, you know, since we got here."

"I do. I know it seems like things aren't progressing fast enough. But we had to find a suitable place. One we can work with. This isn't exactly the most conducive to long-term survival."

"Exactly." I snapped my fingers. He got my point. Lev was a long-term thinker. We were on the same page or close to it.

Lev stared down at me. "I know that look."

"What look?"

"You want to leave."

"It's been two weeks."

"Nila, it is not a vacation. You can't just pack up and go."

"Yeah, we can," I said.

Lev shook his head. "You do this, you know. Leave the cabin, don't leave the cabin, go to Canada, come home. I didn't want to leave the cabin in the first place. You wanted to come down here and maybe chase the rumor of the survivor camp in the Keys."

"It's not a rumor, it's true," I argued. "We talked to them, what? Weeks ago."

"And you don't want to go."

"I just kinda think being on an island is boxing yourself in if there's trouble. And this place, you just said it's not conducive."

"It's not going to be easy to grow food. But we are far enough from signs of the infected."

"We haven't seen any at all since winter. It's over."

"It will never be over, Nila, not when Canada is battling it," Lev said. "Look, if you want to leave and find somewhere else, we will. But for Katie's sake we need to stop. To settle. We cannot be nomads moving about constantly."

I could see it wasn't going to go smoothly with him. I ran through possible comebacks, what I would say. I could tell him that Marco Island or city, whatever it was, wasn't the place to be. The beach wasn't even that nice. It had seaweed everywhere, shells, dark sand. It had a feeling of being marooned on a deserted island.

"Nila," Lev snapped his finger in front of me.

Did he just snap at me? "Lev, don't snap at me."

"You were day-dreaming."

"I was thinking of a response." If I wasn't frustrated enough before, I certainly was now and that was coupled by the fact he looked calm. "You know you said we can't be nomads."

"I did."

"Why not?"

"Why not?" Lev laughed. "One, we would never know our surroundings well enough. Two, we would be scraping by. I don't want to scrape by. Three, gas. How are we going to get there? It's been just about a year, gas will not be good for much longer."

I flung out my hand. "Oh."

"Oh, what?"

"That's not true."

"Gas going bad is not true?" Lev asked.

"No, there were plenty of shows on television that showed survivors years later using gas."

"That's a TV show."

"Still," I argued. "You would think they did their research."

"Nila, a fiction story isn't always fact. Gas will be bad very soon."

"How do you know?" I asked. "Did they test it?"

"Yes, I am sure they did. Why are you arguing so much with me?"

"It's the heat."

Lev exhaled. "Listen, I will do what you want to do, as long as the others agree. Let me know before I start working on the cabin. Okay?"

I nodded.

"I'm headed back to the car. We'll leave the beach soon." Lev turned. "I don't know why we left home in the first place."

I watched him walk away then peered at my daughter. She had wandered a little down the beach, and I called out a warning not to go too far and to stay away from the water.

She looked at me and waved, so oblivious to everything. Nothing seemed to faze her anymore, good or bad.

I peered to Fleck. "What do you think?"

83

"I'll do whatever."

I knew Bella would want to leave. Of course, I'd ask her. I couldn't see her saying 'let's stay' as she complained often.

Leaving and going further south was a bad idea. Other than Fleck's family, we didn't even pursue one of the reasons we went to Florida and that was to find the survival camp in the Keys.

I didn't trust it.

I stopped trusting anyone outside our group.

Hell, I rarely spoke to the people at the campsite.

I looked back to see if I could spot Lev. He had disappeared over the crest of the beach. I suppose he was annoyed with me; I was annoyed with myself.

I thought about his statement that he didn't know why we had left home in the first place.

So much had happened and enough time had passed that I had a hard time remembering why we had chosen not to stay.

I shielded my eyes from the sun and looked at Fleck. "You ready to leave the beach for—"

A scream.

Bella's scream.

Naturally, I turned to look at her, then I heard Fleck.

"Holy shit."

Through my peripheral vision I saw him jump from the lifeguard's chair.

I spun to see where he was going. My heart dropped to my stomach, immediately thinking Katie had been pulled into the water.

Never did I expect to see my daughter crouched down by the water's edge, oblivious to the fact that an infected had come out of the ocean and moved her way.

"Katie!" I tried to scream, her name getting stuck in my throat as I raced forward.

It wasn't easy running in sand, especially on a beach that hadn't been maintained for a year. There were rocks and branches and other debris that made my charge forth for my daughter impossible.

I couldn't run fast enough. My ankle twisted, I felt something jam into the bottom of my foot.

It was like a bad dream.

The way it moved, the way it pushed forward through thigh-high water aiming for my child. It moved with agility and it moved fast.

"Katie! Run!"

It was seconds, I know it was, but it seemed like an eternity.

Katie slowly stood up, looked at me, then turned around and looked at the infected. She didn't scream, she didn't run, she backed up slowly, staring at him.

Fleck was trying to get a shot but it wasn't safe for him to fire. Katie was too close.

"Come to me," I yelled, but before she could react, I arrived, sweeping into her like a linebacker, grabbing onto my daughter just as the infected reached her. I swung her around and out of the infected's way, tumbling to the ground, and landing as the single shoot was fired.

I looked up, still shielding Katie.

The infected flew back, then after he landed in the water, he got back up again.

"Jesus Christ," Fleck blasted, racing toward it. He nailed it in the face with the butt of the rifle. It didn't even seem to faze him.

Fleck hit him again and again until it looked like he'd gone down. It was brief.

I saw the infected come out of the water slowly, then I realized it was a different one.

I jumped to my feet, grabbed Katie and hollered, "Just shoot them!"

During my run back, Katie in my arms, I hollered for Bella to take the baby to the car, and then I called out for Lev.

He had to of heard the shots. How could he not?

I saw him hurrying over the crest, carrying a rifle in one hand, a pistol in the other.

"Go." I moved Katie toward Bella. "Go with Bella."

"Are you gonna kill them, Mommy?" Katie asked

"Go!" I spun around just as Lev arrived handing me the pistol.

My back had been turned from the water for only a few seconds, but when I faced the ocean again, Fleck was backing up as at least a dozen rose from the water making their way to shore.

I may not have been a fast runner, but I was a good shot and I wasn't pissing around.

There was no time to worry if they were infected or dead, or where they had come from. I would take the kill shot, and that's what I did.

TWELVE

BEGIN AGAIN

We had become complacent. Despite how much Lev and Fleck verbally disagreed with me, they knew in the back of their minds I was right. It had been so long since we truly were confronted by the danger of the infected and deaders that we had stopped looking over our shoulder. Being on watch was a formality to us instead of a necessity. We were off balance. Our reaction time to the situation wasn't where it had been six months ago.

Even though we all said it wasn't over, I don't think there was a single one of us who didn't want to believe it was. The lack of infected and dead meant the outbreak was done. The threat was over.

Obviously, by the bodies on the beach it wasn't.

They were fresh.

Several lay on the beach having made it to shore, while a few floated back out after they were shot.

Three days earlier I wouldn't have thought twice about leaving Bella, Katie and Christian in the car. Now I was antsy.

"Can we go?" I asked. "Please."

"They came from the ocean, but where did they come from?" Lev questioned, staring down at them as if he didn't hear my plea to leave.

"They floated," Fleck said. "Maybe they were out there a while."

Lev shook his head. "No, we know that the deaders fall apart, if they were out there, the sea would have broken them down. Look at them."

Not a single one of them was bloated or waterlogged. They didn't have any of the skin tears. "They aren't deaders," I said. "They're infected. Look at their skin." I reached out to nudge one with my foot and Lev quickly stopped me.

"You're bleeding."

I glanced down to my foot all covered in blood. "I must have stepped on something."

"Well, don't touch them," Lev instructed.

Fleck nudged one of the bodies. "The skin isn't soft or mushy. It's firm."

"Infected," I repeated. "They operate on memory. Either they floated until they were close enough to swim, or they fell off a boat. It has to be something like that. They're all fresh."

"Which means," Fleck said, "phase one has begun all over again. The virus is back."

Lev slightly shook his head. "Sadly, I don't think it ever left."

Katie was beyond enthusiastic in an almost disturbing way as she told Ben the story of the infected in the water.

"He was trying to move. But you know how it is moving in water. It's hard," Katie said.

"Is she serious?" Ben asked.

She beat us to the punch and gave him the low down.

"You're saying about a dozen of them?" Ben asked. "On the beach?"

We nodded.

"They weren't bloated?" he asked.

"No," I answered. "They looked like infected. Not deaders, infected."

"Impossible."

I lifted my hands—I didn't know what to tell him.

He asked if either Fleck or Lev could take him to see the bodies, and I told them I was fine with the kids, and to go. I was curious what Ben would think.

They took off but before they did Ben told me not to touch the fish. At first I thought maybe he was insinuating they were contaminated, but then I realized it was another reference to my cooking.

I took it upon myself to inform those down in the Meadow Area about what happened at the beach. Surprisingly, they were pretty dismissive about it. Taking it with a proverbial pinch of salt as if it was an isolated incident.

"Probably just were floating in the water for a while," one man said.

"You know how they are, they don't die."

"Last hurrah."

"Ha-ha."

Um, it wasn't a joke.

The first thought that came to mind was to reach out to Westin, but the Meadow Area radio guy said only Grace in town could do that. She operated out of the local station.

She was only there until sundown.

Great.

I returned back to our cabin area, and while I still felt it was safe, a part of me was on edge. Suddenly my security net was gone and I was constantly looking out, listening for any movement, sniffing for any smell.

When Ben returned he seemed shaken.

"It doesn't make any sense whatsoever," Ben said. "None. There were seven bodies on the beach. Three more were walking the beach when we got there."

"Walking?" Lev asked with sarcasm. "Only until they saw us."

"So they were infected?" I asked.

Ben nodded.

"Were the three on the beach ones we shot?" I asked.

Fleck shook his head. "No, they were new."

I exhaled. "So they're still coming."

"Like I said," Fleck added. "It's back."

"And like *I* said," Lev argued, "it never left."

"No," Ben said. "You both are right. We saw fifteen people, all infected, all in the same stage of the virus. You could tell by the skin, the black veins, all of it. Same stage. Which means they all caught it from the same source. Not long ago they were all sick. If there were fifteen there are more."

"How can that be?" Lev asked. "Could one infected have bit them all?"

"Did you see any bite marks? Ben questioned.

"I…I didn't look," Lev replied.

"I did. I looked. Not one had a bite mark. Nothing. They weren't bit," Ben said. "They all caught our virus. Just like the first outbreak."

"Maybe they were on a boat," Lev said. "Maybe they caught a fish that was contaminated by an infected."

"Or maybe the means of transmission have changed," Ben said. "And another outbreak has started. Either way, they were all together when they got it. Fifteen people, they came from somewhere. Question is, where?"

If anyone would know what survivor groups were around us it was Grace, the radio lady in town, or Westin.

Lev and I hightailed it to the radio station to catch Grace before she left.

Like those in the Meadow Area, she held an air of disbelief. As if we were crazy, making it up. Though I understood her hesitation. After all, no one had seen any deaders or infected in some time.

Finally, after she made it clear she was annoyed with our presence she agreed to make contact with Cobb Corner. Carl answered and made us wait until he got Westin.

"And you're sure?" Westin asked.

"Positive," I answered. "I'll take Ben's word on it, he's a doctor."

"Wait, honey, you have a doctor?" Grace interrupted with a completely switched tone that was sweet and upbeat.

I waved my hand at her. "Oh, so now you want to be nice to us."

"Nila," Lev scolded softly.

"Just that I have this pain in my shoulder—" Grace said.

"Tough," I cut her off.

"Nila," Lev said stronger.

I returned to speaking to Westin. "Sorry. I'm back. Anyhow, Ben thinks they all caught it at the same time and in the same way. We just don't know where they're coming from. We're hoping you might know of a camp that was in this area."

"Well…" There was a pause, a snap of static and Westin exhaled loudly over the radio. "I hate to say it. I think I have a good idea. We haven't heard from Key West in over a week."

"That's a hell of a distance to float in the water," I said.

"Not if they left by boat," said Westin.

Grace tapped my arm. "They're cut off. They guard their ports and bridge pretty good. No way. It can't be them."

"Grace said there's no way," I told Westin. "They're too cut off."

91

"One way to find out," Westin replied.

He was right, there was only one way to find out for sure, and that was to go to the Keys and see for ourselves. Not that I wanted to go to an island of the dead, but it was so important to know. If Key West, shut off from everything, was indeed infected, then there was the possibility of a second outbreak and nowhere was safe.

THIRTEEN

STAYING AFLOAT

May 25

Despite the emergence of infected out of the ocean, it still was a safe place to be. At least I felt that way when the decision came to leave Katie, Bella, and the baby at home or take them with us to the Keys.

In the end I opted to take them with us. I didn't trust strangers, and to me, nice people or not, they were still strangers to me at the campsite.

In exchange for an ear irrigation, which by the way was pretty disgusting, the Marco resident allowed for Ben to use his yacht. It was much nicer than the fishing boat he lay claim to.

Having lived his life by Lake Erie, Ben had been a boater and knew what he was doing. He knew we had to leave early in the morning to avoid the westerly winds.

It would take us approximately three hours.

Grace told us that we would see the port that they used as their official check-in point, and that we shouldn't use any other or there would be problems.

I didn't worry about that, none of us did. There were problems in the Keys already, I knew it and felt it.

We tried radioing them while en route but we didn't receive any replies.

Westin was certain the infected had come from Key West.

They were coming from somewhere near water. We saw several more in the water as we made our journey.

Infected and deaders floated by, all of them reaching for us as if they had some exceptionally long arms and could snag us from the boat.

With Ben at the helm, Fleck sat nearby armed and ready. Bella went below with the baby, and Katie sat on deck with her tablet, drawing away.

The wind from the ocean felt good. The cool mist masked the heat. I sat on the deck watching Katie, and Lev sat next to me, arm on the railing, staring out.

"Look, Mommy." Katie held up her drawing. "I drew you and the ocean deader."

Her drawings were getting better, still a step above stick figures. "That's wonderful, sweetie, but it was an infected, not a deader."

"Nila." Lev turned to me. "Why are you encouraging this?"

"She's being creative."

"Have you seen her drawings?"

"Every one of them."

"They're all twisted and demented."

"Lev, they're all of what she has seen." I raised my eyebrows. "Do you expect her to draw a happy house with a smiling family?"

"Yes. She's five."

"She's living in a different world."

"Doesn't that scare you?" Lev asked. "Wouldn't you rather shield her?"

"I'd rather do whatever it takes to make sure she stays alive. If she knows reality, she'll be a survivor. If we color over the truth with flowers and butterflies, she'll never make it."

"I understand that."

"She made a Lev book."

"A what?"

"A Lev book. She wrote a book about you," I said.

Lev looked taken aback. "A book about me?"

"Don't expect a literary novel, she's five. It's a picture book."

"Still. I don't know what to say."

"Wait until you see it." I turned to my daughter. "Katie, did you bring the Lev book?"

Katie looked up. "In my book bag."

"Why don't you show Lev," I said. "I bet he wants to see the Lev Book."

"He won't get mad?" she asked then turned to face Lev. "You won't get mad at me?"

"Why would I get mad?" Lev asked.

"For drawing you without asking," Katie said.

"That's fine," Lev told her. "I am honored you would write a book about me. I would love to see it."

"Okay." Katie scooted on her hands and knees, pulling her pink book bag forward and reaching inside. She pulled out a pile of papers, shuffled them into a neat stack and handed them to me.

"Don't you want to read it to Lev?" I asked.

"You can do it, Mommy, I want to finish my pictures."

"Okay, baby, thanks." I moved closer to Lev and showed him the first picture. "This is us. Me, you, Katie, Corbin, Sawyer and Billy all going to Canada."

"Why am I so big?"

"To her you are." I moved to the next one. "Oh, look you're sad in this one. Billy's gone."

"Do I want to see the next…"

I switched to the next picture.

95

"Oh, Nila."

"This is Corbin, see how sad I am. Look how angry you are."

"I see."

"And this is…"

"What is all the red?"

"Blood," I explained. "That's you beating up the soldier. And this one…" I switched the picture.

"Is me getting my ass kicked. I can see the big eye I have. What are all these lines underneath?" he asked.

"Words."

"They're lines."

"She's five. She doesn't know how to write real words yet."

"Maybe that's what we should be focusing on. You know a psychiatrist would have a field day with this…"

I readied to move to the next drawing when I felt the boat slowing down. "Why are we stopping?" Holding the pictures so they wouldn't blow away, I stood up. I knew we weren't anywhere near the Keys. "Ben?" I called out and walked toward the front of the boat. "Ben, why are we…"

I didn't need to finish my sentence. My question was answered. Four boats were floating ahead of us. Two were small and the other two were yachts that were comparable in size to ours.

What made it frightening, though, was two of them, the larger and one of the smaller, had infected onboard. The second they spotted us they rushed the rails. Some even jumped into the water.

The other small one appeared empty, until the infected began to react to us, then a lone infected sat up, and he too jumped into the water.

"You may want to move it," Fleck shouted.

"I'm on it," Ben said.

Lev grabbed his weapon and rushed to the side of the boat ready and aiming at the infected as they made their way to us.

"Oh my God," I heaved out a fearful breath. "They're swimming."

One of the infected grabbed ahold of the outer wrung, just as the boat jolted and picked up speed, leaving it in the wake of the boat.

One held on, until Lev shot her and then she released and dropped in the ocean.

I watched the body get further from sight as we moved full speed ahead. "They weren't sick when they boarded, I bet. They were escaping. I bet they were. All of them on boats, trying to get away and evacuate."

"From where?"

"Where do you think?"

Lev faced the empty ocean. There was nothing but sea in front of us, but before long we would be at Key West and we know for sure if they were the source of the infected evacuees.

FOURTEEN

THE KEY TO IT ALL

The Florida Keys were made up of many islands but at least we knew which one for sure had shut down all access roads. We were told Key West was the main island, and that a haven camp had been set up on Big Pine as well.

I don't think it mattered.

Even at a distance we could see a halo of thick dark clouds lingering over the islands. Like something taken out of *King Kong*, hidden bodies of land.

The closer we drew the more boats we saw. A large ferry was just floating, moving along with the motion of the water. We didn't have a clue how many people were on board. Or rather, infected.

We kept a distance, looking at the islands through the magnified lens of binoculars.

Fires still smoldered; the docks were strewn with bodies.

They didn't just have a few infected gone mad, they had an outbreak and the chaos that came with fighting to survive ensued.

We moved as close as we could—keeping a safe distance away, but close enough to see, then after we were satisfied we had our answer, we turned around, heading northwest back to the mainland.

"When I was in New York," Lev spoke to us as we slowed down to a near drift as we neared port, "people would get sick. Hospitals filled up with those who had the virus. They weren't bit, they caught the virus, caught it and turned. It was quiet until they started to turn."

"That's the way it was in Erie," Ben said. "That's when we ran to the boat."

Fleck nodded. "We never really knew that the actual flu victims were turning. No one did until it got out of control."

"One or two at a time," Lev said, "can be controlled, but when you have hundreds upon hundreds getting sick and turning at the same time, it gets out of control."

Ben stood up and started pacing. "When the infected became violent, we all forgot the origins of the virus."

"I don't even remember," I said. "And my brother gave me the heads-up long before things went south."

"Did it stop is the question," Ben said. "Did the virus die out or was it just buried beneath the infected?"

"Stay inside, stay alive," I said. "People hid. They fractioned off. Smaller groups were less likely to catch the virus."

"How many were in Key West?" Lev asked. "Westin said thousands."

"Fortunately, they're far enough away," Ben said. "They won't make it to the mainland before they decompose enough to not be a danger."

"More than a dozen already did," I said. "Those boats will land somewhere."

"Again," Ben said, "not before nature wears them down."

Lev shook his head. "We experimented. Lester lasted a really long time. I think the virus mutated. I don't know the medical or scientific side of these things, but that makes sense."

"I don't either," I added. "But I know there still has to be a source. If you put a hundred virus-free people in a quarantine, away from everyone and then suddenly they get sick, it has made its way from somewhere. The air, mice—"

"Birds," Fleck interrupted. "I'm telling you it's the birds."

99

"Or mosquitos," I added. "I think it's them, too."

Ben tilted his head with a wave of his finger. "Could be. I heard Fleck mention birds before. I am starting to wonder if you're right."

"What do we do?" I asked. "What now? I mean…is there anywhere even safe to be or go?"

The moment I said that, I heard it. It was faint at first, away in the distance, but enough to cause me to stand. When I did it was louder. I turned my body to the sound and everyone else did as well.

It started as a speck in the sky and grew bigger and louder as it came toward us from the west.

A helicopter.

It grew incredibly loud and it flew low and over our heads, never slowing down, never even acknowledging us.

We all looked at each other in shock. Did it come from Key West? Or somewhere else.

All I knew was the helicopter seemed to be headed in the same direction as we were.

FIFTEEN

FLIGHT OR FIGHT

There was this ridiculous fear in me that the infected, somehow, were flying that helicopter. They had jumped from the boat and swum to get us and so the argument on whether they were motivated by memory, to me, had been solved.

They were. They must be

What was to say they weren't flying it?

It was ridiculous; the more I thought about it, the more stupid I felt. After all, if there was a helicopter full of infected, surely their inability to control their rage and go after us would have caused them to drop that chopper right by us.

There were a lot of theories tossed out on our boat. Who they were, where they came from, what they wanted. Obviously, not us.

We had to remind ourselves it had been a year since we all, in one way or another, had retreated to solitude and safety. None of us truly had a clue what had happened to the rest of the world.

Every pocket of survivors was isolated, most of them staying informed by a former chief of police in a small Virginia town.

Our first order of business when we got back would be to find Grace and radio Westin to let him know Key West was dead. Not that we knew a hundred percent for sure, but we knew enough that it wasn't a safe haven.

The threat was back, or rather, according to Lev, forefront again because it had never left.

The question was what our group was going to do next. We needed to find a place that was safe, away from large groups and conducive to long-term survival.

Ben steered the boat back to the dock, anchored then tied it. We made a pact that we would all sit and discuss what our next course of action would be.

The wagon and bike waited for us and we piled in. Katie seemed unphased, napping as if she had taken an afternoon vacation.

It was still early in the day so Grace would still be at the station. I thought we'd try there on the way back to camp. We pulled up to the station, but the door was locked.

"Is she not here?" Lev asked. "It's only three o'clock."

"Maybe she had something to do," Ben suggested.

"Biggest problem in this world right now," Lev said. "No one has anything to do. Our daily lives are spent either doing nothing or finding things to keep us busy. Grace has one job." He looked over my way, seeing the look on my face. "What is it, Nila?"

"I'm just worried. What if this outbreak is airborne and it's just hitting everyone? What if it's the air we breathe?"

"As a medical professional," Ben said, "I can assure you that is not the case. The virus was airborne, that was how it spread so quickly, but that doesn't mean it's in every molecule that we breathe."

"So, where's Grace?" I asked.

"Maybe taking a nap," Ben said. "It won't make a difference whether or not we radio Westin today or tomorrow. Let's just go back and have that talk about options over dinner."

Reluctantly I agreed. What choice did I have?

We returned to the campsite and settled in. I took Katie into our little cabin to allow her to finish her nap on the couch. Ben had an idea about something he wanted to make for dinner, while Lev and Fleck went to the Meadow Area to inform those down there about what we saw at Key West.

Christian was fussy; he cried constantly and for the first time in a long time I worried about how far his cries carried and if it would put us in danger. The more I thought about it, the more vulnerable I felt. We had no safety measures in place at the campsite.

I sat on the couch with my hand on my daughter's back, feeling her take her sleeping breaths, when Bella walked in. Christian squirmed in her arms, letting out little whines here and there.

"Hey," I said. "What's up?"

"Can you take him?" she asked. "I don't know what I'm doing wrong. He just won't stop fussing."

I stood up from the couch. "Is he hungry?"

"I already tried. He won't take a bottle or the applesauce. I'm just tired, I think he senses I'm stressed."

"Probably." I brought him up to nose level and sniffed.

"I just changed him, he's good."

"He doesn't feel warm. He might be teething."

"I just need a break."

"Absolutely. Stay with Katie? I'll take this one outside and walk him."

"Thank you."

Often I forgot that Bella was still a teenager, and that she took on this monstrous role of being the baby's mom. It wasn't an easy task, and we as a group did what we could, but the bottom line was the responsibility rested mainly on Bella.

She handled it well.

I believed she focused on Christian as if he were hers because she had no one else in the world.

"No problem." I held Christian in one arm, allowing him room to place his head on my shoulder. He brought his legs up quite a bit and whimpered. It was possible he was sick from the traveling.

I hoped that was all it was.

103

Fortunately, we had Ben. He always downplayed everything.

I stepped outside the cabin and walked back and forth on the porch.

I peeked through the cabin window at Bella who had rested her head back on the sofa. She took on most of the responsibility for Christian and it was a lot on her.

I wanted to stay close and not go too far. I thought maybe walking the baby around the patio with some fresh air would help.

He quieted down and his body drew heavy, telling me he was falling asleep.

I was about my third lap around the patio when I saw Lev emerge from the path. I could tell by his face something wasn't right.

"What is it? What's wrong?" I asked, approaching him.

He looked over his shoulder, moistened his lips and then looked back to me. "We need to get our things together. I'm going to suggest going to Cobb Corner. At least for a little bit. Even then I don't know if that will help."

"Lev, what are you talking about?" I asked. "What's going on?"

"They're gone."

"What?"

"The people living down at Meadow Area...gone. All of them. Not there. They took their stuff, packed in a hurry...gone."

As if in some sort of protection mode, I held the baby tighter. The infected on the beach, the infected on the boats, Key West, the helicopter, Grace not around and now those in the Meadow Area were gone.

Something was going on and I wasn't quite sure I wanted to stick around to find out what it was.

From the moment we discovered the people in the Meadow Area were missing, we decided we would stick together. No more parting ways to do a run, or to check something out. Every one of us went together. That included heading back into town immediately to the radio station.

We were cautious. Even though we knew we were returning for the night, we packed a few things in the wagon, just in case.

Fleck was able to break into the station through the back door. Grace had used a generator to power the radio but it wasn't running when we got there. We powered it up and then the station.

A cup of coffee sat on the desk before the radio along with a half-eaten bowl of soup.

Grace was having lunch and never got to finish it.

Something was amiss.

"Here, let me." Ben took over the radio operator seat. He ran his finger down a list on the wall. "This is the frequency she used to talk to Westin." He tapped it, then reached for the dial and stopped. "Okay, that was the last call she made out." He brought the microphone close to his mouth depressing the button. "This is Marco calling out to Cobb Corner, do you read? Over."

Nothing.

Oh God, I thought, *don't let them be gone as well.*

Ben repeated the call.

It seemed bleak until a rush of static came over the airwaves.

"This is Cobb, Westin..." His transmission broke up with static. "Who is this?"

"This is Doctor Ben."

"I'm sorry you're breaking up."

"Ben," he repeated. "And you're breaking up too."

"You guys okay?" he asked.

"Yes. Listen we went to Key West. It isn't good. They're infected," Ben said. "People are missing from here now."

"I would ask...repeat." Triple clip of static. "But I got it."

I looked at Lev. "What would cause that?"

Ben replied to me, "Interference. Maybe a storm somewhere." He returned to the radio. "We think we're headed up that way. Do you copy?"

Nothing.

"Westin?"

It wasn't just another rush of static, his entire message was garbled with it. "Listen," Westin said. "Whatever...do...don't—"

More static.

A lot of static, and it seemed as if that was all.

We kept trying, but we had no luck.

"He was warning us about something," Ben said. "I'm sure of it."

"Maybe they're infected," I said.

Ben shrugged. "I would think he would have known this morning. It's something that occurred while we were on the boat."

"So what do we do?" I asked.

Ben swiveled the chair around. "I still say our best option is heading back to Cobb Corner. I know"—he held up his hand to Lev—"you want to go to the cabin. I get it. But we need to stop somewhere and find fuel. Cobb Corner is our best bet."

"I already said the same thing to Nila," Lev said. "I agree with you."

Fleck asked, "What if the warning was not to go there?"

Lev sighed out heavily. "I guess we'll find out."

FIFTEEN

FROM LEV'S SIDE

May 26

It was a long night. One that was difficult and unnerving because every sound caused me to worry. Fleck and I switched shifts keeping watch. While one was on a roof, the other packed the wagon.

There would be no rest for me. I had Fleck sleep during the last couple hours. We'd leave at first light. I encouraged Nila and Ben to rest because they'd have to drive if need be.

Cobb Corner was nine hundred miles away and taking the back roads, like we did when we'd traveled south, would add even more time on to our trip.

I estimated it would take at the very least sixteen hours. Which meant, even leaving at dawn, we'd have to find somewhere to spend the night.

We took mainly state highways and two-lane routes, steering clear of the interstates.

Those roads took us through a lot of small towns.

Just before we stopped for the night, we passed through a small town on the border as we crossed into North Carolina. Grassland, I believe. I didn't recognize the name and was certain we hadn't passed through it on our journey southbound. Surely we would have noticed the bodies?

Bodies lay on the road, outside of stores, some cars looked like they'd just been abandoned where they stopped. Not many, about eight, had their doors open. It was a smaller scale scene of the chaos I had seen before, left over from the original outbreak. But something about this town was different.

"Lev, why are you stopping?" Nila asked, leaning between the seats.

"Fleck did," I answered.

"Okay, so why is he stopping?"

"I think I know."

"Want to share?" Ben asked.

I lowered my voice. "These bodies don't look that old. None of this does."

"You're right," Ben said. "I'll go with you and look."

"Stay put, please," I told Nila and grabbed for the car door.

"You're leaving us in the back seat?" she asked. "I hope the child locks aren't on."

"Mommy, look at that cat eating that body," Katie said. "Do you think he knew that person? Maybe it was his owner."

I paused before getting out. "Can you…can you have her not look out the window, please, thank you."

I stepped out and closed the door, walking around the wagon to meet Fleck. "Why did you stop?"

"You notice anything strange about this?" Fleck asked.

"It looks fresh," I replied.

"Exactly," Fleck said. "Look at these cars, they're packed up like they were leaving." He walked over and peeked inside one. "We should siphon."

"We can do that," I said.

"Lev, Fleck," Ben called out. "Can you come here?"

Ben was crouched by a body.

He peered at us as we approached him, squinting from the sun. "Infected. No bite marks. Necrosis has started. Single shot to the head."

"All these people were infected?" Lev asked.

"I only looked at a couple. They were shot, too. This one I looked closely at. Infected, and um, here's the strange thing. He was infected, but I don't think he turned."

"You mean into a deader?" I asked.

"No, I mean into the raging infected. This guy was just sick. The skin color tells me that."

"What about the others?" Lev asked.

Fleck's voice was a little distance away—I hadn't even noticed he had walked away from us. "This one's arm," Fleck said. "Barely any spider veins."

Ben raised his eyebrows. "How about that?"

"So the people that lived here, and it looks like there were maybe twenty or so, they were sick and they all got shot?"

"I'd have to look at every body but that's a possibility," Ben said.

"We don't have time. Let's just get gas while we can and get going. That way we don't have to stop again before Cobb."

Ben agreed and stood. We needed to leave this town.

We traveled north, making a pact that we would stop when we felt it was too much. Fleck, hating to admit it was too tired and felt unsafe on the motorcycle. So we stopped before I would have liked to.

Keeping us out in the open exposed was not an option, not with everything going on. Unfortunately, it was the only option available to us. We stopped on a bridge that gave us a clear view of anything should it come our way.

It was a restless night for the kids, but we were back on the road and nearing Cobb Corner before eight the next morning.

About a quarter of a mile before the town, the road started to wind before finally opening up. We hit the bottom of the small grade with Fleck still riding a short distance ahead of us, and I could see the brake lights on his bike through the morning haze as he took the final bend.

I thought at first he was stopping to wait for us, but then I saw the real reason. Two military vehicles and an unmarked white utility van were blocking the road.

"Lev?" Nila called my name as I hit the brakes.

I mumbled softly, "Turn around, Fleck, come on, turn around."

"What's going on?" Nila asked.

"I don't know."

Fleck began to turn the bike when I saw two people in white biohazard suits carrying military-style rifles halting him.

I placed my hand on the gear shift and prepared to go just as three more people in hazmat suits walk up to Fleck. Those three weren't armed and their suits were yellow.

"What are you doing?" Nila placed her hand over mine on the gear.

"We have kids in this car, Nila. We can't go any further, especially if the virus is there."

"We can't leave Fleck."

Ben said from the back, "We can't stay."

I saw through the corner of my eye Fleck stepping off the bike and raising his hands.

All that ran through my mind upon seeing the guns and the hazmat suits was that place we'd driven through in North Carolina. The cars with the doors opened, the people shot lying on the ground.

"We have to go." I placed the wagon in reverse but before I could hit the gas, a triple pounding knock on my window instantly caused me to freeze.

110

A man in a white bio suit aimed the rifle at me. "I need you all to step out of the vehicle."

I just stared at him, trying my best to think of a way out.

Another armed man approached on the passenger's side.

Again, the man at my window repeated his request. "Step out of the vehicle now." He paused. "Please."

I wound down my window and spoke in a low voice. "Look, we have children in the car. Can you step back and lower your weapon? You're scaring them."

"I'm not scared, Lev," Katie called from the back seat.

I utterly cringed at that moment, shot a glance to Nila, then looked at Katie in the back who was peeking around curiously.

I looked again at the person who stood at my door. He lowered his weapon and stepped back. He did as I requested, and we really had no other choice but to do what he had asked in return.

Reluctantly, we stepped from the car.

SIXTEEN

LET'S BE CLARE

The town of Cobb Corner was just up ahead and I worried, if they, like everyone else had gone or worse...dead.

For as scared as I was, for some reason I slipped into some weird survival mode. We weren't going down without a fight.

Maybe I had the killer instinct after all. But when the soldier or whatever he was backed away from the car, I was able to switch the safety off my pistol and make sure the semi auto switch was engaged. As I slipped from the car, I placed it behind the waist of my pants. The blood rushed to my ears. I inched my way around the front of the car, back sliding against it to be near Lev. He opened up the back door, reached for Katie and held her.

It had to be what had happened in Canada that made him clutch my daughter.

"Lev?" I whispered.

"I don't know. I'm just...thinking of that town."

"Oh my God."

"Stay close to me." He looked behind him to Ben and Bella. "We all stay close."

"If anything," Ben said, "anything remotely goes wrong. Bella, I want you to take Christian and run. Run as fast as you can."

"No worries," she said. "I will."

"Nila, do you want to hold Katie just in case you have to run?" Lev asked.

"No, I'm the best shot here. Trust me, I'm ready. I can take out three of them before they get off a single shot."

"Mommy's funny," Katie said.

"This way," the man said, walking before us and leading the way.

"No one is behind us," said Ben. "That's a good sign."

Lev grumbled a "hmm."

We walked until we met up with Fleck.

"They say anything to you?" I asked Lev.

"Nope, just that I can put down my hands," Fleck answered.

We stood in a group, close together as those armed formed a wall before us.

It was hard to distinguish through the suits if they were men or women; the only indicator I had was the size of the body and height.

What I believed to be two men walked up to Fleck. One had a clipboard, the other some sort of instrument. It was white and it reminded me of one of those grocery store scan guns, only winder.

He held it to Fleck's face, waved it in front of him, then instructed, "Tilt your head to the left." He scanned his neck. "To the right."

Fleck did.

"Hands please, palms up." He ran the tool over them. "Palms down. Thank you." He turned to the man with the clipboard. "Clear."

"What am I clear of?" Fleck asked.

"No signs of the virus," the man replied.

"I could have told you that."

"Not if it's early on. Next."

He repeated the same actions with every one of us, with the same monotone instructions. Each of us was deemed clear.

"Why all this?" Ben asked.

"Just protecting the town, sir," was the answer we received. "We apologize for the inconvenience."

"Is this for good?" Ben asked. "You weren't here when we passed through before."

"No, it's not permanent. We're searching." The man with the clipboard moved forward. "By chance have any of you received a scratch or a bite from someone sick and did not contract the virus?"

It was déjà vu. Canada all over again. A man with a clipboard asking that question. There was no doubt in my mind about how I was going to answer.

I shook my head *no*, but I knew, I knew it was coming.

"Me," said Katie cheerfully.

Before anything could be done, the second I saw the rifleman make a hair of a move, I whipped out my pistol and placed it to the clipboard man's head. "I swear to God, touch her and I blow his head off. Try it."

The man with the rifle raised a hand, moved his rifle to the side and raised the other. "Ma'am we have no intention of hurting the child."

"Please take the gun from my head," Clipboard Man said calmly. "We're not asking so we can hurt her."

"So you're not responsible for those bodies in that town a few hundred miles back? All with bullet holes in their head."

"We probably are," Clipboard Man said. "But they were infected, I assure you."

"The whole town?" I asked.

"No, just those people. We rescued about seven who weren't. Those we shot were ill, some in the early stages, some not. I assure you they had the virus," said Clipboard Man. "Entire groups are getting sick. Please take the fucking gun from my head. Our interest in the girl isn't to harm her, it's hopefully to help us stop this."

"Nila," Lev said calmly. "Lower the weapon."

114

"No, Lev, I don't trust them. If one of us wouldn't have been clear, they would have shot us."

"Yes, we would have," Clipboard Man said. "I'm being honest with you. We have to stop this thing by any means necessary but that does not include killing a child who could possibly be immune."

Ben stepped to me and in front of Lev, sandwiching Katie between them. "Lower it, Nila. They won't harm her. They have to go through me and him. And we know he's tough to take down."

It took a lot, but I did. I lowered the weapon.

"Jesus," Clipboard Man gasped out. "Thank you."

"Can we go to our cars and go into town?" I asked.

"Yes," he replied. "We'd really like to talk to you. It would benefit your group. You can trust us."

"It's kinda hard to trust someone whose face you can barely see," I said.

A woman's voice called out. "You can see mine." She stepped forward. "Can you take a moment to talk to me? Just you." She looked directly at me. "Please."

That's when I saw Westin was with her.

Lev moved forward. "Westin, what is going on?"

"They picked up my radio transmissions," Westin said. "They're looking for life and people."

"They're shooting people," Lev told him.

"Lev," Westin said. "I may not agree with what they're doing, or how, but they are trying to stop this virus before it wipes us all out. Or turns us into a world of those things."

"Who are they?"

"Those mythical beings called The Colony," Westin replied.

"Actually…" The woman, wearing a hazmat suit as well, walked up to me and extended her hand. "The Colony is a place. I'm Clare." She shook my hand.

"What did you want to talk about?" I asked.

"She's your daughter, right?" Clare pointed to Katie.

"Yes," I said. "Can he come too?" I indicated too Lev.

"If he's the father, then yes, he can."

"He's the father," I replied.

"No," Katie sang out with a giggle. "He's not my dad, silly. Daddy was the one who bit me."

Silence filled the air.

Then Fleck spoke up. "Okay, you know what?" he said. "Someone really needs to teach this kid the old adage that children should be seen and not heard, or maybe...try some duct tape on her mouth."

I really wanted Lev to go, father or not, and I told her I would only speak to her with Lev present.

I had Fleck take care of Katie and warned him jokingly not to duct tape her mouth.

"Okay, here's where we stand." Clare exhaled as she sat in her chair behind a desk in an office set up in the rear of her utility van. She wasn't old; she was actually young. I was willing to bet she wasn't a day over thirty-five. Her brown hair was pulled back into what I would call a messy bun. Strands dangled around her very tired face. "When we picked up the radio signal coming out of this town we intercepted and made contact. We found out Westin is pretty much the person people check in with. People that haven't made their way to a Colony."

"To be honest," I said, "no one really knows about The Colony or where it is. We just learned about you recently after we heard some people have been looking for it."

"They find us or we find them," she said. "So as I was saying, knowing that Westin makes contact with people from all over, we figured maybe he had heard from your group. He had. We had a team in the area checking out Key West. The radio woman told us where you lived, but you weren't there."

Lev asked. "Why were you looking for us?"

"We retrieved a lot of intake information from Canada before they fell. Several instances were documented of people that were bitten and survived. Of those coming in on the Ontario border, your group was one of four." She opened up a folder. "You had a man named Corbin with you."

"He was killed by them," I said.

She nodded. "I saw that. Ignorance isn't always bliss, is it?"

"He was straightforward," I told her. "He thought maybe they could use him. Maybe there was something special about his blood."

"And there was," Clare said. "So knowing that your group was ejected, we were hoping to find a family member. And we found him with one of the other groups."

"He has a son," Lev said. "Sawyer. They kept him and wouldn't let us take him."

"Oh, we located Sawyer," she said nonchalantly. "He's with a family in Colony One. He is not immune though."

I gasped out in shock and then smiled. "Sawyer's okay? He's alright? Lev!" I reached out and grabbed his arm. "Wait until we tell Ben."

"There was another little boy with us. Billy," Lev explained. "Any word about him?"

"No, I'm sorry. There was no mention about your daughter being bit either," she said. "Again, we were just hoping for a family member. Your daughter, if immune can be a great help."

"Are you forcing people to go with you?" I asked. "Because everywhere we have stopped or been lately people have either gone or there are dead bodies."

Clare shook her head. "We're not forcing anyone. They came and joined us of their own accord. The people here at Cobb Corner

117

aren't joining. Well, they aren't relocating. They'll be a sort of hub for us. Some people want to go. And, yes, we are killing those infected. We have to. We have to stop it by all means necessary. This time it's spreading faster than the first one, and we still can't figure out how it just pops up in some areas and in groups who haven't been exposed to anyone."

"Birds," I said matter-of-factly. "Birds or mosquitos."

"A dog spread it in my camp," Lev said.

Clare produced a closed mouth smile. "Yep. It appears to be everywhere and anywhere. We would like you to come with us to Colony One. You don't have to stay for good but I think you'll like it."

"How many Colonies are there?" I asked.

"There were five. We lost a colony to the virus and infection two weeks ago. We had to seal it off," Clare said.

"What exactly are the colonies? I mean, if you want us to go with you, you need to tell us more," I said. "Are they camps? How do you guys have the means to trucks, gas…research?"

Clare shook her head. "We're not camps. We're cities. I worked for Federal Emergency Management. Way before my time there, I think it was twenty years ago, the administration started Project Justin. It was a plan to ensure the continuity of mankind should a catastrophe, outbreak or anything similar occur. Named Justin for just in case. Five cities were designated as Colony points. Once the event began construction and planning would go into effect to create the perfect environment in the city for whatever the event was. In this case being viral, it meant sealing off all but one entry point, creating boarders and building walls. While cleaning up inside."

"How long ago did you finish?" Lev asked.

"About five months ago. Everything was ready to initiate and we began doing so right away." She looked at me. "I know this sounds crazy, even far-fetched, but these cities had been prepped for decades. Teams were always on call. Thousands of people were involved. We lost a lot to this virus, but we also gained new people."

118

"And you want us to go?" I asked.

"We need you to go," she said. "We aren't looking for a cure. We need a vaccine to create immunity. That is what we are trying to accomplish. Colony One has our research facility. That's where those who have shown immunity live. Your daughter's cooperation is very vital, especially since she was bit."

She wanted us not only to consider whether we would go, but to answer right away.

I still didn't understand exactly who these people were. Was their presence a confirmation that an arm of the government was still operational?

Did we want to be a part of that world again?

We had a decision to make, not one easily rendered at the makeshift office in the back of a white van. We as a group were a family, we lived together, traveled together and even though Katie was my daughter, it was a decision we would make together.

SEVENTEEN

THE BAND

June 6

It was on blind faith alone that we decided to go, though still unsure that we weren't lambs being led into slaughter. It was trusting the face and word of a woman who we had met after being held at gunpoint. It was all because I wanted there to be a world for my daughter when she grew up. Not a world full of infection.

We respectfully and politely turned down the transport they offered, which entailed meeting up with a convoy outside of Washington D.C.

I didn't want them to have that much control over us. After all, it wasn't prison. They said we would be free to go if we wanted to after a few blood tests.

If they were able to use or needed Katie more, they asked that we remained where they could find us.

Colony Two was located in east Texas, a shorter journey than Colony One which was in Burlington, Vermont.

Clare and her people mapped out our route, which would take us along all major roadways. She told us we would see fuel trucks and help stops every few hundred miles.

Previously, we'd avoided using major highways, though if we hadn't, we would have learned about The Colony long before we did.

We stayed another day in Cobb Corner, then started to make our way north. Bella and Christian stayed behind and we left the solar generator for them. Ben came along but only to find Sawyer and said he wanted to return to Cobb Corner. He liked the idea of being a town doctor. Fleck…I didn't know. A part of me thought we were going to lose him to Colony One. Not lose as in death, but he always said he wanted to find people.

I knew we would all head back to Cobb Corner one way or another. In fact, we made a pact that should we by some chance get separated, we were to meet up at Cobb.

Twice we stopped for the night at one of those refueling places or 'help stations' as some called them. Not that we needed it, but they gave us water and a meal, and Lev was finally able to get a good night sleep knowing someone else was on watch.

No matter where we stopped, if it was a Colony outpost, they scanned our face, neck and hands.

They were nice at the posts and treated us with respect.

Most who worked at them wore military uniforms and one of the soldiers even told us he had known about Project Justin for the entire ten years he was in the service. He had been on call for the project and had attended various drills.

It was crazy how planned out it was. And no one had ever known; it was such a closely guarded secret.

Our final overnight was just outside of Sarasota Springs where our directions had us leaving the main interstate and taking a series of secondary highways.

Before Sarasota, we'd see an occasional car left on the road, but after…it was clear.

The route had been maintained and kept safe.

It was hard to believe that the virus had returned again full force and we were starting the illness to infection stages all over. It was like being back in a nightmare. We had finally thought we'd found some kind of peace…that nature was finally balancing out again and we'd be able to start over. How wrong we'd been.

There was a sense of peacefulness until we hit Shelbourne. Then we heard gunshots cracking off occasionally. We thought we were too close to Colony One for there to be infected, but we were assured we were safe.

We knew we had arrived when we came up to a fenced-in section of the highway, which started right before a four-story hotel. It was there we were told to park; no civilian vehicles were permitted in Colony One.

There was another reason for pulling over in the parking lot of the hotel—it had been made into some sort of receiving center for newcomers. Even though we didn't bring much, we were told to leave our bags outside and they'd be returned to us.

They did let Katie keep her little pink bag in which she carried a couple of toys.

When we stepped inside the hotel it was like part one of leaving the apocalypse.

Fleck let out a sigh of relief. "Ah, AC."

Ben turned left to right. "They have power. Do you think it's a generator?"

"They're running a lot for only a generator," Lev said. "I mean why waste it on AC?"

"And coffee." Fleck pointed across the lobby. "There's coffee."

The small lobby had been turned into a reception area, reminding me so much of Canada. Lobby furniture had been removed and replaced with more tables where people were filling out papers.

There were several people ahead of us, and by the time we reached the desk, Clare came out from the back.

"I've been waiting for you," she said, then instructed the gentleman doing intake to give us the paperwork. "It's all part of the process, even if you decide not to stay. If you don't mind..." She pointed to a table. "Just find me when you're done, I'll personally take you through the process."

Fleck got us all coffee, and I savored mine as I filled out the paperwork that was similar to a job application. When we were all finished, Lev took them to the counter and a few moments later, Clare returned.

"We'll get you all settled and into your rooms," she said. "But there is a process that we go through. First is a blood test to determine level of immunity and your general health." She led us down a hall. "You'll get one of these." She held up her hand exposing a yellow bracelet. It was a wide band that looked like it should hold one of those exercise watches. "I'll explain these later."

"So we're staying here?" I asked.

"Until tomorrow, then we'll move you all to temporary housing in Colony One. You'll stay there until your permanent housing and job details are finalized, or until you decide to leave."

"I'm here to find Sawyer," Ben said. "I want to find him. I have known him since he was born. He's no less than family and I want him back."

"I will work on reuniting you," she said. "Right now"—she opened the door to the room marked Ballroom 1—"tables to the left do blood work. They'll send it to me right away. When you're done there"—she turned—"that woman over there will give you some personal effects and toiletries to hold you over. Then you wait. And we'll try to get your results as soon as possible to get you moving." She glanced down to her watch. "I'll catch up to you soon, I promise. You missed breakfast, but lunch is at one. You should be done by then."

After she walked out, Lev leaned down to me. "Okay, this is a little ridiculous."

I gave him a hush face then twitched my head down to Katie. She clutched her pink bag looking around.

"They're trying to find that one person," Ben said, "who can stop this all. So they're thorough. I expected Canada to be the same."

It didn't take long for them to take our blood. Katie was a champ. Of course they let her look around and grab items from the one table that was filled with books, crayons and paper. She shoved them into her bag and I swore she left it open on purpose to see how much more she could take.

They separated us, telling us we'd see Fleck and Ben at lunch.

We were taken into an office near the ballroom. A stack of clear plastic storage drawers were on the wall by the desk. It was only as tall as Katie and I kept having to ask her to stop touching them.

It was the longest I believe we had waited since we'd arrived there. Lev and I sat in the chairs facing the desk, the items we were given on our laps. It was unnerving. Finally, a woman walked in. She seemed slightly out of breath and rushed.

"I am so sorry," she said, then she paused and caught her breath. "My name is Doctor Hillgrove. Pleasure to meet you both." She shook our hands. "And that is Katherine."

"Katie," I corrected. "Where's Clare?"

"Oh, she'll join you soon. I am, however, very excited." She walked over to the stack of drawers, opened three one at a time, pulling something from each drawer. Katie watched her and she smiled at my daughter. "Can I see your left hand?"

Katie lifted her right.

"The other one," Dr. Hillgrove instructed, then looked at me. "As we suspected, Katie is immune. One hundred percent to everything. The viral strain and the mutations found in the infected and the passed. This"—she lifted a light blue band—"is for you." She put it on Katie's wrist. "It'll take a day to get used to. It's kind of bulky." She winked. "But it lets everyone know how special you are." Leaving Katie, she walked to us. "Nila."

"Yes."

"The gene is passed on genetically. Since your husband died of the virus, as did your father…" She lifted a chart. "Brother and daughter." She paused. "I'm so sorry."

"Thank you."

"You," she said as she reached for my wrist, "are immune to the viral strain." She placed a green band on me. "Which means, airborne, blood borne, no matter how that virus is transmitted in its original form, you will not get it." She locked the band on me.

I examined it. It had a snap latch and I moved my wrist around.

"However, you can still get it if you get bit or scratched," she said. "Hopefully, that won't happen. Extreme measures are taken to stop those who are ill from turning. Levon." She had one band in her hand and I could see the yellow color of it. "This is for you."

Lev held out his arm.

"Wait this is too small." She walked over to the drawers. "Excuse me, honey," she said to Katie, having her step out of the way. "Large are on the bottom. I wasn't thinking." She grabbed another and returned to us, placing it on Lev. "These bands let the authorities know about you. I understand you three will be together. But I must tell you, should there be an emergency, should there be an evacuation, those bands are crucial. First ones out are blue and green. They'll separate you. I'm sorry."

"We don't plan on being here that long," Lev said. "So it's alright that I'm not immune. They are."

"That is sweet." Dr. Hillgrove smiled. "Now, you'll just…" Her head turned. "Oh, honey, no, no. Don't touch those."

"Katie come here." I held out my hand.

The doctor was very nice, but still my daughter gave her this evil look that I didn't understand as she slammed the drawer, clutched her pink bag and moved to me.

Dr. Hillgrove cleared her throat. "As I was saying. You can go wait in the dining area and Clare will show you to your rooms. We can't make you stay. We would ask you to stay for a few days so we can run some tests, collect some more blood, and a tissue sample from you and your daughter. Uncomfortable, but vital to the research. Will you think about it?"

I nodded. "We came here to help. So we'll stay to do that."

"Thank you." She walked to the door. "Who knows, you may like it here."

Lev laughed once as he stood.

While Dr. Hillgrove gave him a lost look, I understood why he laughed. It was a sarcastic reaction to me. Lev told me I was unsettled, that I wasn't going to like it anywhere we went. As we made our way to the dining area, I had a feeling that Colony One wasn't going to be an exception.

EIGHTEEN

WINDOW

Yellow.

When we met up with Fleck and Ben in the dining area, which, naturally, had been set up in the restaurant, they both sported yellow bands like Lev. They didn't seem fazed by their lack of immunity until they saw I was a fortunate one.

Lunch was pretty basic: soup and a sandwich. After that, Clare showed us to our rooms and said she had to go back into the city for work.

Our bags were already in the room, and thankfully no one had stolen the bottle I had brought. Immediately, I poured a drink.

I never would have thought I would feel uncomfortable being back in a world of technology. We were out of our element on the road, but even more so in the hotel.

It wasn't so much a hotel experience. We were responsible for our own dishes after lunch and were told cleaning the room after we left was our responsibility as well.

The next day we would be taken into Colony One where, as promised by Clare, Katie would get special treatment. We both would and because Lev, Fleck and Ben were with us, they would benefit as well.

Clare already started her push for Ben, to keep him at The Colony because he was a doctor, but he was steady and firm that he was there only for Sawyer. Katie was excited about Sawyer as well.

Even though we had adjoining hotel rooms, we all sat in one. After we all had taken turns basking in hot showers, there was nothing else to do. Katie watched DVDs on the television, Fleck fiddled with his yellow band a lot as he paced to the window, staring out.

"Everything is back up and running," Fleck said. "You can see the lights. They have power."

"Technology breeds comfort," Lev added. "I wonder how many people are in Colony One."

"By the looks of the lights," Fleck said as he turned from the window, "a lot."

Ben shook his head. "If there is a viral outbreak, it's going to be a repeat of what we lived through."

"What do you suppose they meant when they said they had to seal off one of the Colonies?" I asked.

Ben shrugged. "They shut it down, I guess. Got out who they could."

Her little feet kicking as she lay on her stomach and watched the television, Katie blurted out, "Bet they burned it down like the island."

"Katie, why would you say that?" I asked.

"Because she doesn't have a filter," Fleck said. "She saw a burning island. Not long after a helicopter flew over. She's smarter than we think."

"Come to think of it," Lev said, "if Key West had been out of commission for days, how were the fires still burning?"

"But Key West wasn't part of the Colonies," I replied.

"Come on, Nila," Lev said. "They have no limit on the extremes they will go to to remove any and all infected. It doesn't matter what stage they are in. We saw that."

Ben sighed when he sat on the end of the bed. "At least they were getting people out."

"With the right bands." Fleck looked down at his.

"Were they?" I asked. "Look, I don't know what Colony One is going to be like, but I don't know if I like the idea of living scared to death of getting a fever or sniffles."

Everyone looked at me.

"Okay scared for all of you to get the ordinary flu."

"You're right." Ben walked to the window to join Fleck. "They won't take any chances. With that many lights we can assume there are hundreds of people, and with the virus popping up out of nowhere, there is no way Colony One is infection free."

At that second we heard two shots in the distance.

"It's either here or close," Ben said. "I don't want to live through all of that again."

Fleck walked away from the window. "Maybe we're jumping the gun here. Clare said we'd like it. It would be good for us. We're on the outskirts of Colony One. We don't know."

"No, we don't." Lev stood and walked to the dresser, pouring himself a shot's worth of booze. "But...tomorrow will tell." He downed his drink. "Tomorrow will tell."

NINETEEN

LOST AND FOUND

June 7

Was the nightmare over? The moment the van left us at the corner of Main Street after taking us through the fences, I felt like I had stepped into a science-fiction movie.

How did we go from living day to day, running from the infected, bathing in a creek to a picture-perfect clean environment? People walked the streets drinking take-out beverages. Those who got out of the van with us had the same expression. Confusion.

Did such a perfect place really exist?

Were those who lived in Colony One truly as oblivious as they looked or had they just chosen to forget the horrors they had faced?

Colony One barely looked as if it had been the fall of civilization. Some of the local businesses were closed and boarded up, while others were being worked on.

Was it possible to live here? To be one of those people sipping a green drink while laughing with a friend walking nonchalantly down the sidewalk. Could we successfully pretend a dead world didn't exist?

Yes, as long as you ignored the fences and never looked beyond them.

Clare gave us a laundry list of details as she took us to our temporary housing.

"We exist because people work hard to keep it that way. Everyone has to be a productive part of this society. Everyone has a job, everyone pulls their weight."

I didn't want to tell her I was the queen of jobs—I just had a hard time keeping any of them.

A large portion of the city had been knocked down to make way for farming and greenhouses. They were located out of the safety zone and workers commuted there every day.

There were three safety zones. One encompassing the university medical center where most of the research was being carried out; the second nearby which was a residential area; and the third was the main and biggest section consisting of six square blocks with City Hall Park being the center point. Those blocks were surrounded by large fences. Buildings had been demolished, creating piles of bricks and rubble to keep people at a distance from the barriers and fences. What lay on the other side was a polar opposite of what was within.

On the inside everything was clean, it had beauty and life. On the other side was an overgrown world with shattered buildings and burnt-up cars—an uncomfortable reminder of the violent death that had swept through.

I wondered how many people went to the fences and looked out. If, of course, they could get close enough to see around the rubble.

We'd seen it because we drove through it. It was like waking up from a nightmare. Only Colony One wasn't a reality, it was a ruse. A ruse to those who lived there.

Those were my thoughts.

We spent a good part of the day, Lev, Katie and I, at the medical center. It was simple testing. When we left Fleck and Ben in town, they were waiting to get into the temporary housing. Ben was getting antsy. He was desperate to see Sawyer. He told Clare he was almost to the point where he was going to walk around town calling out Sawyer's name. It wasn't that big of a place, he'd find him.

Clare told us at the medical center that the family that had taken in Sawyer was leery about us.

"Who cares," I told her. "His father would have a fit if he knew he wasn't with us."

She relented and said she would take us after testing.

I was worried about Sawyer. What had he been through since I last saw him? I even thought maybe they'd lied to us, that Sawyer really wasn't there. That was until we pulled up to the cute little two-story house in the secured residential area.

We had barely stepped from the safety van when Sawyer barreled through the front door of the house screaming, "Ben! Ben!" and ran straight into Ben's arms.

The look on Ben's face said it all, his emotions poured out as he lifted and cradled Sawyer tightly against him.

"I'm so sorry." Ben kept his mouth near Sawyer's ear as he said, "I am so sorry for what you've been through. So sorry I wasn't there."

"It's okay. You're here now."

Ben set him down and Sawyer ran to me and hugged me.

"Hey, buddy, we missed you."

"I missed you guys too." He stepped back and looked up to Lev. "You're alive. I thought they killed you."

Katie said, "It sure looked it, didn't it?"

"Yeah."

"Oh, Jesus," Fleck commented. "Two of them now?" He smiled and walked to Sawyer. "Glad to have you back."

Sawyer turned. A man and a woman stood on the sidewalk before the house. "The Stewarts took really good care of me."

Ben approached them. "Thank you, I appreciate it very much."

"We're sad to see him go, but happy he has his family back."

"Is he okay?" I asked. "I mean with all he's been through."

"He's doing great. He really is."

I placed my hand on my chest and exhaled in relief. "I'm so glad to hear that."

The goodbyes to the Stewarts were a little longer than the van driver wanted, but Sawyer and the Stewarts needed that time. His things were already packed and ready to go so we left after the good-byes.

I suppose I had been too nervous and excited when we first drove to see Sawyer, or maybe they weren't there, but I missed something vital on our way in. When I noticed Lev sit up and turn fully to the window once we pulled away from the gates of the residential area, I took notice.

This stretch of road was open and vulnerable to anything, especially since they had torn down a lot of the properties.

"What is it?" I asked Lev when I realized something had caught his attention.

"Look." His finger tapped against the window.

There weren't many, and they looked more like stragglers, but they were definitely there and too close for my comfort, right there by the residential fence...infected.

TWENTY

DATE NIGHT

The temporary housing resembled more of a YMCA shelter than anything else. Our special treatment consisted of us having our own room lined with bunks.

It didn't matter to the kids and that was the only important thing. They were either naïve about everything or immune to the horrors.

There were a lot of kids in the building, but I didn't want them to mix and mingle. Staying away from others was vital, especially with a silent killer like the virus.

The two of them sat on the floor and Katie immediately shared some of her drawings with Sawyer.

"Dinner," Fleck announced when he walked in. "For the kids. Adults have to wait until a later time to eat." He set down a plate with sandwiches and two bags of what he said was milk. "Peanut butter and jelly. It's been a while since any of us had that."

"We had peanut butter and jelly at the cabin," I said.

"No bread, Nila. You need bread to make a sandwich," Fleck said.

I shrugged and glanced at Ben. He was only watching the kids. I walked over to Lev who was on the bed. "You alright?"

"Yeah, just..." He sat up and swung his legs over. "Worried, you know. I want us out of here. As soon as testing is done, we leave, okay?"

"Absolutely. Hopefully they'll take us to the car."

"Yeah, hopefully. If more of those things gather, walking won't be easy. It's like they smell us."

"Just like Fleck with the peanut butter and jelly. Sniffing out the food supply."

"That's not funny," Lev said.

A knock on the door preluded its opening and a man in a uniform stepped inside. "Evening folks, my name is Captain Marshall." He stepped inside. "Everyone getting acclimated?" He didn't wait for a response. He walked by the kids, rubbing his hand in a friendly manner over Sawyer's head, then placed a clipboard on the table. "I just came to drop off a list of work openings that we have in case you feel one of them is for you. And a map of the area." He held it up and looked around. "I heard one of you is a doctor?"

Before Ben could say anything, Katie did. "He is!" She pointed to Ben.

"What did I tell you?" Fleck asked. "Kids should be seen and not heard when around people they don't know."

"It's fine," Ben said. "I am. But we aren't staying. We came so those two could donate whatever the immune need to donate, and for Sawyer, the boy. We are family and were separated a long time ago."

"I see," he said, surprised. "Wow. Wish you folks would reconsider. I mean, look around. Talk to people. It's a good place."

"I'm sure it is," Ben replied. "We make it pretty safe wherever we go."

"You probably do," the captain said. "Like I said, look around. We could use the hands." He faced Lev. "Especially you. You're a big guy. Ever consider joining the service or at least security around here?"

"No, not really," Lev said. "I just do what I can for my family."

"Too bad. Out there as long as you have been, bet you're a good shot," he said. "We can use someone with that skill."

Lev chuckled. "You're looking at the wrong person then." He nodded my way.

135

The captain turned around. "You're a good shot?"

"I was the best in the valley," I replied. "Well, when the phrase 'in the valley' mattered. But yeah, I am."

"She's a great shot," added Fleck.

"What do you shoot?" Captain Marshall asked.

"Infected, deaders, animals, not people."

He cracked a smile. "I mean. What's your weapon of choice?"

I shrugged. "Any really. I mean, M-4 is a little heavy, all the Ms are. You want me to do damage, put a 9mm or Glock in my hand."

"Saw her take out an infected at fifty yards," Fleck said. "Right between the eyes. It was at night, too."

"My father taught me to never waste," I added.

"So, uh, what are you doing this evening?" Captain Marshall asked.

It was funny what happened after that question. Lev moved forward, not saying anything. Fleck did this coy, single stride to Lev and whispered as if I couldn't hear him, "Dude's got some balls, huh?"

"Um, tonight?" I asked.

It was like I was the center of attention. Everyone waited to see what I would say. Katie spun around completely to look up at us.

Fleck nudged. "Now Katie says nothing. Go figure. I was waiting on something."

"Yes," Captain Marshall said. "I can use a good shooter at North Four. It's at the end of this area, heading towards residential. We have some infected gathering out there."

"Yeah, we saw them."

"I'm trying to be minimalist with shooters, and really want those who won't waste the ammo. If you're as good as you say you are, we could clear that area tonight."

Finally, Lev spoke. "You want her to go alone with you out there?"

"No." He shook his head. "They'll be a few others. I understand, you can call Clare. She told me she has a special interest in you guys. She's perfectly safe with me."

Ben laughed. "Call Clare? And how are we supposed to do that?"

Captain Marshall reached into his back pocket and pulled out a phone. "Only works in this area, but still. You can call her. She's in my contacts."

Ben actually took the phone and stepped away.

"They checked our weapons," I said. "I don't have my gun."

"I'll arm you."

"Are the rest of us invited to go?" Lev asked.

"Are the rest of you as good of a shot as Nila?"

Ben returned pretty fast with the phone, handing it back to the Captain. "Clare says Nila is safe with him."

I actually wanted to do it. And I knew I'd be safe with him. I was immune, they weren't taking chances with me. I was told that. But I also wasn't stupid. I hated the fact that they took my piece, and I really wanted it back.

"So what do you say?" he asked. "I'll swing around and get you about eight?"

"Find my pistol they took and you got yourself a date."

"Dude," Fleck laughed.

"You know what I mean." I shot a glare at Fleck. "Don't instigate."

"I'll find your weapon." Captain Marshall stepped back. "And the rest of you, take a look at those jobs. Have a good day."

The moment he stepped out and the door shut, Lev, Fleck and Ben just stared at me.

I wanted to blast them with a 'what' but instead I silently walked away, joining the kids on the floor. If they couldn't see what I was doing and why, I didn't want to explain it to them.

Until we arrived at sector four, I didn't realize how long it had been since I had smelled the dead so close. The stench permeated the air. It was thick, and I was grateful the temperature wasn't sweltering.

It was still light out—the sun was just starting to set—and I could see them. They hadn't notice us, yet.

The fenced-in area blocked off an older residential street. One of the houses had yet to be demolished. The yards were tall with weeds, and a few cars remained on the street.

Lev was not happy with me; he didn't say anything, but I knew my friend well enough to know when he was pissed.

He started distinctively leaving out his contractions, something he always did.

"I am fine. Just promise me you will be careful. I do not want to have to come looking for you," he said.

Yep. Mad.

When Captain Marshall, or rather Sean as he later told me to call him, showed up, he immediately handed me my weapon. I was glad and showed Lev. He still wasn't getting it. I was armed again, and I had no intention of not being unarmed ever again, especially in Colony One.

I kissed Katie goodbye, along with Sawyer. I wasn't sure how long we'd be out for.

Sean brought a Colony phone and handed it to Ben and said, "In case you're worried about your wife. You can call."

"Thank you," Ben replied. "I will, but she's not my wife. So no worries."

"Oh good. You guys look like a tough crew, don't want anyone chasing me down when I have her out late," he joked. But I don't think Lev understood the humor, nor did he laugh.

He stood up and walked toward us. "How late?"

Sean shrugged. "Hard to tell. But we'll call if you want."

"I do," Lev said. "We will worry. She hasn't been away from a member of our group since the outbreak."

"Really?" Sean asked. "Then this might be a nice change of pace for her. We'll keep you posted."

One would think I was leaving my family for good the way everyone watched like sad puppies when I walked out. Everyone but Katie, who was fine with it.

Sean was right about one thing. It really was a nice change of pace.

It hadn't hit me until Lev said it—since I'd arrived at the cabin, I hadn't been away from the group, our core group, since it started. Someone was always with me.

Sean said he packed some food in case we were out a while, and beer for later if we took out enough infected.

"How many are you taking out daily?" I asked.

"Ten, twenty. A few months ago it was one or two a week. But over the last three weeks it has been steadily increasing."

"Any idea where they're coming from?"

"Nope. And we went out looking."

I checked my weapon and readied it, then looked beyond the fence to the infected. "When do you want to shoot them?"

"Whenever you know you can get a clean a shot."

I glanced out, there were four. One of them was looking for something near the front stoop of one of the houses, while the others kind of meandered their way. They didn't look like deaders, but they moved slowly. Maybe they just weren't inspired to rage toward us. After all, they were still part human, they got winded and tired.

The one by the steps was clearly looking for something though.

"Have you checked the houses out there?" I asked.

"I'm sure we did at one time."

"No, recently?"

"Why would we do that?"

"To see if they are any in there. Maybe a group."

Sean chuckled. "Like they moved into the neighborhood?"

"Or lived here before," I said.

"I get it. Some say they move on memory, but they aren't the Phased."

"The Phased?" I asked.

"The ones that went from sick to the next phase."

"Aw, okay, we call them Infected."

"They're all infected," Sean said.

"Yeah, but that's just what we call them. Then we call them Deaders once they become the rotting kind."

"We call them SACs."

"SACs?"

"Slow antagonistic corpse. SAC."

"You military with your acronyms," I said. "Funny how people have different names for them. Anyhow, they aren't SACs or Deaders, they are Infected. Ragers, whatever you want to call them."

"They're dead." Sean pointed. "We're out here talking and they aren't even running for us. An...Infected would."

"They will. Watch." I raised my weapon, placed my sights on one and fired. He went down.

"Nice shot."

It didn't take long for the noise of my gun to wake them up and once I'd fired they came running. I shot again, taking out another and then a third just as he got to the fence.

The fourth one was still looking.

"That was really impressive."

"It's my gun," I replied. "It makes it easier. What do you suppose he's looking for?" I walked close to the fence.

"I don't know. I'd suggest we find out, but..." Sean pointed as he joined me.

More Infected appeared. They seemed to come from behind the houses and raced up the street.

"I thought you said ten or twenty a night," I said. "There's at least twenty."

"Yeah, I see that."

"Does it worry you?"

"Yeah." He raised his weapon. "Yeah, it does."

TWENTY

FROM LEV'S SIDE

The nightly entertainment was at my expense. The moment Nila left with that captain they started joking about it with me. Trying, I guess, to get me. It was immature but at least they were laughing.

They had it wrong.

I wasn't worried about Nila going off with this captain in some sort of prelude to a romantic night. That wasn't Nila. I knew her well enough to know. My concern had nothing to do with jealousy, it had everything to do with my fear that Nila would be seduced. Seduced into a new lifestyle, that she would want to stay in Colony One.

That was my biggest concern.

I paced a lot, watched Katie work on her drawings. She shared them with me, told me what they were, even though I could clearly make out the images.

I thought about using the phone to call Nila. I studied that phone to see how it worked but I decided against it. I didn't want to be overbearing.

Everyone passed out early except me. I went from pacing to lying on the bunk to getting up and looking out the window. A cycle I repeated.

Until finally, the phone rang.

It had been so long since I'd heard a phone ring, it caused me to jump. And the forgotten familiarity of the phone caused everyone to wake as well. I answered it on the first ring, keeping my voice low. "Hello."

"Hey, Lev," Nila said.

"Hey, hold on." I signaled to Ben and Fleck that it was fine then returned to my phone call. "What's going on? You okay?"

"I'm fine. I just wanted to check in. How are things?"

"Good. Good. Everyone was asleep."

"How about you?"

"Not yet," I said.

"Then you aren't trying hard enough. Get some sleep, Lev. It's the only time you can. You're not on watch."

"I've been getting too much sleep lately," I said. "How long will you be?"

"I'll be a couple more hours, we're headed to another sector."

"Is something wrong?" I asked.

"I'll tell you when I get back. I have to go. Kiss Katie for me?"

"Absolutely. Be careful."

"For sure, and Lev."

"Yeah?'

"I love you."

"I love you, too." I waited a second, then ended the call. The phone beeped and I set it down.

I walked to Katie's bunk and kissed her as Nila asked. As I went to tuck her in, I noticed the pink bag she carried. She had it cradled to her chest. It was odd, because for as long I'd known Katie, I'd never know her to be so protective over something.

What did she have in there she didn't want anyone to see? That was my thought. I reached for the bag but stopped. It wasn't my place, nor was it right to peek. I fixed her covers and went back to my bunk.

After the call from Nila, I felt less restless and finally fell asleep.

I don't know how long I was sleeping, but I woke up as soon as Nila walked in. Of course, she made noise, tripping over things in the

143

dark, repeatedly saying, "Sorry" until she sat down on the bunk next to mine.

"Hey." I sat up. "How'd it go?"

"Good. I guess. I'm tired. We went to nine sectors tonight."

"Nine?"

Nila nodded. "You can say I saw a lot of this place tonight."

"And?"

She leaned down to untie her boots. "I saw enough that I think we can't stay here that long. As soon as me and Katie are done, we'll go. It's not gonna be safe, not for long."

"Did you shoot a lot tonight?" I asked.

"Yeah, more than I thought I would."

"Deaders?"

"Infected."

"For real?"

"Yep."

"How can that be?" I asked. "I mean, we barely saw any for the longest time and when we did, they were deaders."

"I have a theory on that." She removed her boots. "You know how there's this bible verse that says, 'when one or more gatherers in my name' or something like that?"

"Book of Matthew, yes."

"Well, I think that's what's happening here. I think when we were a small group we didn't attract them. But here, there's so many people, it's like a beacon. They're going for the beacon, not the small stuff."

"Did you…did you just use the Bible as an analogy to an undead apocalypse?"

Nila facially cringed. "I did. But it's the best way I could think to explain what's happening. Sean says the numbers have been increasing weekly."

"Whose Sean?"

"Captain Marshall."

"You're on a first name basis now?"

"Yeah, I'm working with him. I plan on going out to do this again as long as we're here."

"Can I ask why?" I questioned.

"Because I want to get close to him. I want him to be on our side. He's a good one to know. He's honest." She glanced up at me from the tops of her eyes.

"I take it he was honest and told you some things tonight?"

"Yes, he did."

"Do you want to tell me?"

"I do. But can it wait until the morning? I'd rather not whisper and I'm really tired."

"Nila, you can't just leave me hanging like that. It's frustrating."

Then before Nila could say anything, Fleck's voice came out of the dark. "From what I gather, she's been leaving you hanging and frustrated for some time now."

In a rare occasion, Nila snorted a laugh.

Not wanting to be the butt of any more jokes, I gave up, said good night and whether or not I could fall asleep, I laid back down and closed my eyes.

Whatever it was, Nila would tell me. I was certain.

TWENTY-ONE

TO THE BONE

June 9

It wasn't as if Colony One was a bad place. It wasn't built with bad intentions, nor did it harbor any sinister secrets. The entire Project Justin was good in theory. It would have worked in the event of a normal plague or extinction virus. Not one where the infected can enter a stage of extreme strength and rage and have enough remaining intelligence to open a gate.

I likened the people like Clare to those flashy salespeople, who in the old world would promise you a buffet lunch if you listened to a speech on time-shares. Her and others like her had a responsibility to bring people in. The only way the Colonies would work was if everyone worked to rebuild.

What they didn't tell us or probably anyone else was that a third of the population had lived there before the virus. When they learned the virus was extinction level and Project Justin kicked into gear, they were rescued and placed into safe houses, protected while the soldiers and those there for the project cleaned houses and killed infected.

They were sheltered. Which meant a third of Colony One didn't have a clue how to survive or live beyond the fences. They didn't know how to escape the infected.

Which was dangerous because the infected were closer than they knew.

They didn't seem worried, why would they be? For a year they had been protected. Why wouldn't they still be?

The morning after my first Sector watch, I explained to Lev and the others what Sean had told me. How The Colony that had fallen experienced increased infected, and an actual outbreak within resulted in only twenty-five percent being evacuated.

The rest weren't just sealed in, they did a clean sweep.

Firebombed The Colony.

As inhumane as it sounded, it stopped the virus from spreading to nearby survivor camps.

The entire mission of Project Justin was to save humanity…at all cost.

If the virus isn't contained, if the infected weren't killed, little by little it would infect the world and only the few that are immune would remain.

I didn't talk much about it to Clare when I saw her the next morning at the hospital. Just that I had enjoyed the outing and was interested in doing it again. I even went as far as to lie and say if I had that job, it could influence me to stay.

I was a little miffed when she replied, "Really? I thought for sure you would want a food service manager job."

I guess in a post-apocalypse world, Arby's is impressive to have on your resume.

What I really wanted to know was how long we'd be there. I expected a few days, so my plan to stay on Sean's good side looked promising, until she asked me to donate stem cells.

"You and Katie both," Clare said. "It's vital. We would need you another five days. During which you can't really run around. I would prefer you not to leave at all for a week after the cells are retrieved."

"I can go shoot in the sectors, right?"

"As long as you don't do anything too physical."

"I can sit on my ass and shoot," I said.

Clare smiled. "It's good to have you out there."

"Clare." I folded my hands on her desk, leaning in to talk to her. "There are a lot of people in this place that don't have a clue how to handle an infected."

"We want to have a world where they don't need to," she said.

"Is that really realistic?"

"With the right team members on patrol, it can be. With a vaccine or the right treatment, it will be. If we can save people from getting the virus or stop the virus from turning them into Phased, mankind can eventually render the virus extinct instead of the other way around."

"I understand. And you know, infected are plenty for some reason. You can easily have them captured for testing."

"Unfortunately, the ones running around out there," Clare said, "are too far advanced. Even though they aren't SACs, we only test on those in the early stages before they phase."

"Wait. You only test on…early stages? Test on, meaning present tense. Is the virus in Colony One?"

Clare only looked at me.

"I knew it," Ben said. "I knew it. I knew it. I said it was here. You can't have a couple thousand people in a sectioned off area with those things outside the fences, without it being in here."

"A couple thousand?" I asked. "Eight thousand, four hundred and seventy-three, not including us."

Fleck whistled. "I didn't realize this place was that big."

"It's huge. And it's not the biggest one. Don't ask me, I don't know where the other Colonies are. I do know they are now looking at small towns like Cobb Corner to be subsidiaries."

"Let me get this straight," Lev said. "They're trying to gather up all the people they can?"

I nodded. "Large populations will bring civilization back. The more organized they are the more likely it is they can beat the infection, either through medicine or guns."

Lev nodded. "I get their thinking. But do people actually want that? Do they want to be herded together like sheep?"

"Um, apparently eight thousand people do," I said.

"And," Fleck added, "not everyone shares your passion for avoiding the world and hiding out in a cabin."

"The cabin was and is the best place to be. The property is large. It has room for growth. Earl fortified that place," Lev argued. "Our biggest mistake was leaving there. One day all of you will see that."

"Okay, alright." Ben held up his hands. "It doesn't matter, does it? We're headed back to Cobb Corner. We all decided this, right? I mean it has people and Lev can find someplace to hide. That's the plan. The only solid one we've had for a while. So all of this, the Colonies, it doesn't affect us and is a waste of our energy worrying about it. The only question that should remain is, when do we go back?"

A solid plan.

Ben was right.

We hadn't had a solid plan since we'd all come together a year earlier.

I told them how they wanted to get stem cells from me and Katie and at the most it would be five days. Then I agreed that would be it. If they needed us for anything further they were in touch with Cobb Corner and knew where to find us.

Five days.

We would leave.

At least I was confident that nothing would happen in those five days.

149

TWENTY-TWO

TINY WINDOW

June 13

No one ever told me what all was involved donating bone marrow. In my naïvety, I had never really thought about it. I believed it to be a simple thing, until Ben explained it to me. I was grateful I didn't blindly volunteer my daughter. He told me how they would go into my pelvic bones with needles to remove liquid marrow. And that the stem cell procedure I had been doing for them used to be a well-used alternative to bone marrow back before everything went to pot.

I didn't understand why they needed marrow if they already had been taking an alternative.

But I had agreed and I'd stick to it. I started to get fearful when Ben told me they had to put me under. At that point I told them I was backing out unless Ben was in the operating room with me.

They agreed.

I then had to apologize to everyone because it was going to take even longer. Not only did they want me to wait for the five days after the procedure, I had to wait three days for the procedure while experts arrived from another Colony.

At least they were doing the procedures there and I wasn't some test subject.

They moved us out of the YMCA style shelter to a third-floor, two-bedroom apartment over a former bakery. It was a few blocks from where we had been previously, and it gave us more room.

Everyone took it fine that we had to stay. I enjoyed my three days of sector shooting knowing that I probably would have a hard time after the procedure.

The day of the operation I learned that Fleck truly didn't mind the three days because during that time he had met someone.

Her name was Chandy. Not Candy or Chandra, but Chandy. She came to the medical center with Fleck to wish me luck. That was my first introduction to her. As awful as it was of me, I wanted badly to ask if she was an exotic dancer because she scarcely wore clothing, and what she did wear was barely above underwear.

She was pretty though and didn't come across too bright. Then again, I could have just been nervous and misjudged her. She did, however, seem like the type of woman Fleck would date. Wild and fun.

Lev wanted to stay until I was done, but I told him to take the kids back to the apartment and Ben would come and get him when I was in recovery waiting for the anesthesia to wear off. Reluctantly he agreed, wished me luck, and took the kids.

The hospital was quiet; I didn't really see any patients other than myself, and the staff was minimal. Only a few people walked the hallway. Then again they were doing the procedure late in the day because the surgeon needed to rest after the trip.

They gave me something to calm my nerves. I would have preferred a drink. In the operating room, Ben asked me, "You ready?"

I nodded.

"No worries, you'll be fine."

I looked at him and realized in the year he had been with us it was the first time he acted in a doctor capacity toward me. Those were my last thoughts. I was out.

Ben was the last person I saw when I closed my eyes and the first person when I opened them.

"Hey, everything went well," Ben said.

I could barely focus. I looked around, things went double, blurred. From what I could make out I was in a room, it wasn't huge, but it was too large to be a regular room. But even lying there everything spun.

"I think I'm dizzy." The words sounded slurred. My tongue felt too big and my throat hurt.

"It'll wear off. I'm going to go so Lev can be here. I know he's probably pacing. You'll be fine. You'll only be alone for a half hour maybe. And really you're not alone. You have a good nurse. Right here." Ben pointed. "She'll take good care of you."

I could make out the figure at the other end of the room, but that was it.

"I'm not worried," I said.

Ben smiled and leaned down, kissing me on my forehead. "You did very well. Get some rest."

Eyes barely open, I nodded and passed back out.

When I was married to Paul, I bought this alarm clock online. It was called the Sonic Wake Up. Guaranteed to wake even the deepest sleeper.

It was hard to believe that I was a deeper sleeper now, with the dead raging around me, than I was before everything went to hell. I guess in the old world I had the desire to stay up watching television or watching online video after online video.

The alarm had this echoing, deep buzzer that repeated like a warning and a tiny row of red lights that flashed. Paul hated it. He used to say it woke everyone up but me.

Which was true.

He'd nudge me in bed. Usually the back of his hand into my hip, or he'd poke his bony pointer finger painfully into my butt. "Nila, damn it, shut that thing off," he'd say.

I dreamt of Paul, something I hadn't done in a long time.

Buzz. Buzz. Buzz.

That painful poke. "Nila, come on."

"Stop that, it hurts," I said.

"Shut that off."

Buzz, Buzz. Buzz.

The red flashed against my eyelids.

"Nila, shut that off."

Buzz. Buzz. Buzz,

"Fine." I rolled to my right and a pain shot right through me. I wanted to curse him out for hurting me, but I was too tired. I reached out and shut off the alarm.

Buzz. Buzz. Buzz.

It was my hand swinging at air that caused me to open my eyes.

The light in the room was dimmer. A strobe of red flashing lights blinked steadily in time with the warning buzz.

Reality crossed into my dream. It was an alarm alright, but not the kind that rested on my nightstand.

Something was happening. Was it a fire?

I tried to sit up in bed with a painful stiffness, but as soon as I did, the room spun and blurred out of focus.

Try, Nila, try to see, I told myself.

It was hard. My eyes didn't want to stay open, even though I felt awake. I was conscious and aware, yet my body was too sluggish and felt like it weighed ten times more.

"Hello?" I called out for the nurse. "Hello."

I squinted to see across the room. No one was there.

Immediately, I was hit with an overwhelming and brief sensation of panic. I hated it. It had been a long time since I had felt vulnerable and scared—I was still drugged and half naked.

I could think of a better state to be in.

It was an entire audio and visual experience.

153

The blaring alarm, the flashing red light.

Voices shouted out in the distance.

"Not here. Did you see?"

"No, check down there."

Gunfire. One pop, two.

"Where? Tell me now!"

I jolted and brought my legs over the side of the bed. I was hooked to an IV and I knew that would hinder my movements. I looked down to my arm and couldn't see enough. My fingers probed for the painful spot on my wrist just below my thumb. I could feel the shunt in my skin, taped there.

I cringed as I pulled it out.

I felt the blood roll down my hand, but I couldn't worry about that, I had to get out. Something had happened. Had I been forgotten?

Sliding from the bed, my feet set on the floor and my legs wobbled. I took a step and the floor felt as if it tilted upward.

Everything spun, the walls, the furnishings.

I inched forward, the voices still in the distance, running footsteps, more gunfire. Cooler air hit my back.

It was like walking in a bad drugged or drunk state. I had to focus, find something solid with a line, like a door. I spotted the one at the far end of the room. It was open. I walked that way wanting to get to a wall to hold on for support. Just as I neared the door, I came close to losing my balance when my foot stepped in something thick and wet and I slid forward. It squished like jam under my toes and a sick feeling hit my gut.

I didn't need to look to know what it was. But I did anyway.

I saw the legs, a woman's, encircled by a huge pool of blood.

There was either a madman running around or an infected.

I don't know how it didn't get me. Maybe my sleeping and being motionless saved me.

Immediately I was hit with a surge of adrenaline. I wanted badly to be sober, to be normal, and yet my mind was the only thing that was clear. Physically, I couldn't move fast or see well enough to charge forward and run for my life.

The hallway outside the door was in plain sight and I made my way there.

Mixing with the red flashing lights were bright strobes from the fire alarm system, giving the hall an eerie appearance.

The corridor looked so long. It titled to the right and rippled some. At the end of the hall I could see people running.

Get there, I thought. Make it there.

I staggered down the hall and made it only about ten feet when I saw the three figures at the end.

Hospital workers.

They stood there, arms slightly outward almost hesitant to come my way.

I waved to them. I wanted them to know I wasn't one of the infected. "Hey!" I called out, my voice cracking. "Help. I can't walk."

My voice caught their attention and I realized they weren't hospital workers.

"Oh, shit." I backed up. I didn't want to take my eyes from them, but I couldn't move fast enough. Hell, it didn't matter what way I moved backwards or forward, there was no way I was going to be able to outrun them.

A few more steps, I pivoted my body to turn and just as I did, an arm swung around my waist, latched on tight and lifted me.

For a split second I believed I was in the grip of another infected. As my fist pummeled and legs kicked, I saw through the corner of my eye his arm extended, and he fired a gun.

I knew instantly when two shots landed in the chest of the infected before narrowly hitting the head, it could only be one person that had me...Lev.

155

My body relaxed. He fired at the other two just before he dodged us back into my room and slammed the door. "You okay?" he asked, slightly out of breath as he felt the door. "Damn, there are no locks." He placed his weight upon in. "I think we'll be fine."

The door banged and jolted.

"I think you missed," I said.

"You think?" Lev looked at me and smiled, then tilted his head back to peek through the tiny window. An infected snarled and bit at the window. "Yeah, I missed."

I looked at Lev having never felt so happy to see my friend. He generally looked in a good mood, despite the circumstance. Then it could also have been my medicated state. I felt loopy and dizzy.

"Thank you. You saved my life." I spoke in a whisper.

"You're welcome."

His body bounced as the infected slammed into the door.

"Here I'll help you." I leaned against the door.

"Yes, that will do it. Thank you."

"Wanna hear something funny?" I asked. "There's a dead body in here."

"That's funny?"

"It is when you think about how I was in here too and it didn't get me."

"No, Nila, that's not funny, that's scary."

I gasped.

"What?"

"It's not scary." My eyes focused on the body. "It's Clare. Aw, I liked her." I took a step forward and teetered.

Lev grabbed on to me and pulled me back. "Just stay put."

"I'm having a hard time walking. I guess we aren't making a run for it."

156

"We'll just wait. It won't be long. The soldiers are out there." Lev shook his head. "They'll get them." Again, he tilted back to look. When he did, the infected was still there at the window, and then with a blood splatter, he was gone. "See."

It was a strange rotation of feelings I went through. Scared, worried, hyper then calm. I felt calm with Lev. Then again, it could have been the anesthesia.

Whatever the case with me physically, mentally I was in my right mind and I knew the night hadn't just ended differently than we thought it would, the night and the events of it had undoubtedly changed everything.

TWENTY-THREE

TIME

June 14

In theory, Project Justin was an amazing concept. Be proactive the second an event occurs to secure five cities, reinforce the supplies and prepare for the long term, protect those at all cost, then lock it down.

In application, they had made mistakes. I don't think they'd fore-seen them. Actually, anyone on the outside could not have foreseen what needed to be done.

They had spread themselves thin, operating two, three, some-times four safe zones per city. And in between were veins of existence that had allowed the infected to slip through.

They weren't expecting breaches, but they should have. Nothing is impenetrable. Especially something as invisible as an airborne virus. One person, one sick person afraid to leave their home could trigger a deadly chain reaction.

If I were running things, I think the colonies would be different. Then again, not once did any of us ask who was running things. Who was in charge of the big picture?

Eventually the Colonies would fall, all of them. Not because the invasion would be far too much to handle, but because they would give up far too easily. At least, that is what I got from Sean.

He and his team were first on hand at the medical center. The infected from the sick ward had broken free when they turned unex-pectedly.

Lev happened to be walking in the building. His priority was to find me. Especially when he learned the infected were on my floor.

Not long after Lev brought us back to the room, the power was restored, alarms stopped, and all was clear.

He immediately took me back to the apartment. He didn't wait for them to clean my bloody arm, or even get dressed. He reasoned that Ben was a doctor and he was all we needed. Lev draped a blanket over me, grabbed my clothes in the bag, and off we went.

He carried me until Sean offered to drive us. That was a good thing—not only was I still drugged, my legs didn't want to work.

I slept well that night but woke up extremely dehydrated with a headache that eventually went away with water. I didn't have the pain everyone said I would have. My hips ached a little, but it was more of an annoyance and nothing I couldn't handle.

When I made my way into the living room after showering, they were already having an afternoon pow wow.

"What's going on?" I asked.

Lev turned to me. "I want us to go. After yesterday that is our best option."

"They want me to stay for five days."

"I'm a doctor, Nila," Ben said. "I can watch you."

"Okay." My eyes shifted to Fleck. "This isn't what you want, is it?"

"I don't want to leave Chandy," Fleck replied.

"Then don't. See if she wants to come with us," I suggested. "We'll find a second vehicle. There are fueling stops on the way to Cobb, we'll be fine."

A knock at the door broke up the conversation and Ben walked over to answer it.

Sean stepped in immediately apologizing for the visit. The moment he asked where the kids were and seemed relieved they were in the other room, I knew something was up.

"When do you guys plan on leaving?" he asked.

"We were just discussing that," said Lev. "Soon."

"I think maybe you should go tomorrow."

"What's going on?" I asked.

"Medical moved out," Sean asked. "Not the entire hospital, just the research and everything they are working on. Airlifted to another Colony just twenty minutes ago."

"Is it because of the breach yesterday?" Ben questioned.

Sean shook his head. "No, it's more. Something like this is indictive of an evacuation. It will probably start in three days. Blue and green first, then the rest. You don't want to be here for that. Eight thousand people, and a full evacuation has never been done. Not a planned evacuation. The only other evacuation was at the Colony that fell, and that didn't go well. So, for your safety, I'd leave tomorrow. Ask for a transport to receiving. You'll see a row of military vehicles, Humvees and stuff. They are fueled plus twenty gallons on the roof."

"Jesus," Ben said. "What about you?"

"I'm already on duty tonight in residential. They're moving them into the main area until it's deemed safe."

"Infected?" I questioned. "We know they're out there."

"They're massing. Plus, we have reason to believe there may be infected in the early stages in town. We can't confirm because no one will give up their identity."

"Well, yeah," Lev commented. "You shoot them before you give them a chance. A man named Corbin who was with us was infected. He got sick but he got better."

"I thought you scanned people," Fleck said.

160

"We do. But when you catch the virus, it's different than getting it through a bite. And yes, the scan picks up the infection in the veins before the infected has symptoms. There is also a day or two that they have it where the scan won't know."

"Slips right in," I said.

"Exactly. Just…I'm just giving you the heads-up. You're leaving anyhow, right?" Sean said. "It would be safer for you to leave before the evacuation. If there is one."

"We appreciate it." Lev extended his hand and shook Sean's. "If you're ever in the area of Cobb Corner, you find us. We'd love to have you."

"I may take you up on that. Good luck to you." Sean then looked at me. "And Nila, you keep shooting. It's no wonder your group is safe."

Fleck followed him to the door and closed it. "I resent that."

"We all do our part," Ben said. "No need to feel slighted because he has a thing for Nila."

"True," Fleck said. "Speaking of which. I'm heading over to see Chandy. Take her for a walk."

"Be careful," Ben told him.

"I will."

"So it's settled?" I asked after Fleck left. "We leave in the morning?"

"First thing," Ben replied. "You rest. It's gonna be a long trip."

I didn't feel like resting or sleeping. Not yet. I'd take my mind off of things by playing a game with the kids. There were board games in the apartment.

I was relieved that we were leaving. While I wasn't sold on Cobb Corner, it was a destination and it wasn't The Colony.

I originally had no plans to go to sleep, a part of me was too anxious. We packed up everything we had, which wasn't much, and placed it by the door. Sean didn't really explain what 'transport to receiving' meant; I supposed we'd find out in the morning.

I ended up retreating to the bedroom early. After putting the board game away, I found a box of books and pulled out a murder mystery. I was terrible at reading those types of books, always wanting to jump to the end.

I felt like I was invading someone's home in that apartment. I wondered who had lived there, what they were like. Because of the interior and the way the place was decorated, I thought maybe they were elderly. But the steps were steep and there wasn't an elevator.

That cozy, murder mystery deflected my plans of staying awake. I started to yawn and felt tired. After placing down the book on the bed, I stood to take off my jeans.

Lev knocked once on the door. "You decent?"

"It's a matter of opinion."

Lev came in. "I brought you a nightcap, since Ben doesn't want you medicated anymore." He showed me the bottle. Looped between his fingers were too mugs.

"Oh, awesome, thanks. Join me."

"Sure."

I patted the end of the bed for him to sit.

He extended his hand for me to take one of the mugs. I did.

His eyes shifted. "Were you reading?"

"Yeah, it's a mystery."

"Nila, you're terrible at those."

"I know. It has taken everything I am not to skip to the end."

"Good."

162

"Speaking of which." I reached and grabbed the book, flipping to the end. It took a few seconds of scanning, but I found it. "I knew it."

"Nila." Lev shook his head and poured me a small amount of whiskey. "So I interrupted your reading."

"Actually, I was just getting ready to undress for bed. Try to sleep a couple hours."

"That's a good idea. We all should. Kids are camping on the living-room floor. I thought I'd sleep on the couch so they know I'm there."

"Ben and Fleck?"

"Ben's asleep. Fleck isn't home."

"I figured as much. You usually leave the door open, and when we talk, Fleck makes comments. Do you think he's okay?"

"Fleck? Yeah, I think so. He's with his girl."

I snickered.

"What's so funny?"

"His girl," I mocked. "He's known her for like five seconds."

"You cannot make fun. Sometimes you just know. You know?"

"I don't know. I guess." I shrugged. "Are you alright? You seem off."

"Just everything. Leaving and going to Cobb when we're so much closer to the cabin. I just…I want to go home, Nila. Our home. But we made a deal, a promise. So we go to Cobb Corner."

"I'd break that deal, Lev," I told him, "if it wasn't for Katie. The world sucks as it is. She needs more than just you and I."

Lev nodded, then finished his drink. "You're right. And I should let you get dressed for bed."

"I could do that in the room now, you know. After the little rescue you pulled…" I poured him a splash more. "You've seen me naked."

"Not really. Only from behind."

"No full-frontal nudity."

"Not yet." Lev winked.

"Awfully presumptuous of you."

"Well..."

"Oh my goodness, you're joking."

"I joke."

"No you don't."

"Okay, I don't. Not really. But in all seriousness," Lev said. "Despite the jokes, it's really you and me. It ends up you and me. And...I like that. I hope that one day, we will reach a point where you don't worry about awkwardness or me lying there fretting performance issues."

I blurted a laugh. "You joked again."

"I did." He finished his drink. "I have loved you my entire life. No matter who came or who went I have always loved you."

"I have always loved you too, Lev."

"Not the same way."

"Yeah, I kind of think in the same way. If there is such a thing as a soul mate, you my big friend are it." I downed the remainder of my beverage, and as I brought my mug down, Lev took it, setting it on the floor never taking his eyes from me. He brought his hand up to the side of my face, brushing his fingers down my cheek as he moved in...and stopped.

He just stopped.

"Are you...are you trying to kiss me?" I asked.

He closed his eyes tightly in a wince.

"Wait. Wait. You're doing that *Hitch* movie rule thing. Ninety ten. You go in ninety percent and wait for..."

"You know what?" Lev stood. "Don't worry about it."

164

"Lev."

"No, I'll just go in the other room."

"Lev, stop." I waited until he stopped moving. "You didn't wait for me to go in the rest of the way."

"That's because your mouth was too busy making fun."

"Don't go. Stay. Please?" I held out my hand.

He took a step back toward me, grabbing my hand.

"Wait."

"What now?"

"Close the door."

Still clasping my fingers, Lev extended back his long reach and shut the door.

TWENTY-FOUR

FLEE

The middle-of-the-night civil defense siren wasn't just jarring, it was frightening as it cut suddenly and loudly through the quiet night.

Lev was just getting ready to go to the couch. His hand had barely touched the doorknob when it sounded off.

His expression matched mine. Utter confusion as to what was going on.

He opened the door and threw on his shirt, stepping into the hall at the same time as Ben.

"What the hell is that?" Ben asked.

"I don't know." Lev moved quickly down the small hall to the living room.

Sawyer and Katie were up.

"Lev?" Katie asked, her little voice quivering. "What is that? I'm scared."

"I know, sweetie." He lifted her and turned to Ben. "Where's Fleck?"

"He never came back."

"Damn it."

"Is it a fire?" I asked.

"No, it can't be," Lev said. "It's coming from outside."

I hurried to the window and looked out. Giant event-style spotlights swung through the sky and over the buildings. "People are going into the street."

Lev handed Katie to me. "Let me see if I can find out anything."

"You're going out there?"

"Yeah, I'll be right back," he said. "Stay put." He held out his hand.

"What about your shoes?" I asked.

"I'll be back." He hurried out the door.

"Mommy," Katie called my name.

"It's okay." I set her down. "Let's get your shoes in case we have to go. Okay." I turned to Ben. "Get his shoes on."

"Ben?" Sawyer asked. "What about Fleck?"

"Fleck's a big boy, he'll find us," Ben told him.

I rushed to find Katie's shoes—why was it a child's shoes were never where they were supposed to be? When I finally had them, the door opened. Lev moved with urgency.

"Grab what we can and what is needed. Now. We have to go." He grabbed his boots and immediately put them on.

"What is happening?" I asked.

"It's an evacuation," he answered.

"But Sean said it wasn't going to happen yet. This is sudden."

Lev looked up at me as he finished his boots. "Yes, it's sudden. It's urgent."

"There's been a breach," I said.

"Yes. There has."

"Okay." I exhaled to calm myself, and took the shoes to Katie. "We're gonna go," I said as I put them on. "Alright?"

Katie nodded. "My drawings."

They were on the coffee table along with her crayons and markers. I swooped them up into my arms and took them to my backpack by the door.

"Let's go," Lev said. "They'll be calling for people. At least that was what I was told. If we miss a bus we have to walk. I don't want to walk through a breach. Not with the area bulldozed."

"Nowhere to hide," I said.

"We're ready," Ben announced, standing with Sawyer by the door. He had a backpack across his shoulder.

"So are we. I'll grab the bigger bag. Nila carry the…" He turned. "Where's Katie?"

"Katie!" I called.

"I need Lev," she hollered from the back room.

"I'm right here," Lev replied. "Come on, Katie."

"No," she replied. "I need you to come back here. I don't want to get in trouble."

Lev spun back around to Ben. "Go. We'll be downstairs."

"We'll wait," Ben said.

"No. Go. We'll find you."

Ben nodded quickly, then holding Sawyer's hand they ran out.

"Katie." Lev moved with haste toward the bedrooms. He looked in the first one, so did I, she wasn't there. And in my room, I almost didn't see her. She was hunched on the floor by the bed, clutching her pink bookbag.

"Katie." Lev held out his hand. "Let's go. Don't worry. Don't be scared. I'll carry you. But we have to go. What's wrong?"

Her little eyes watered as she looked up. "You heard them, Lev. You heard the lady. She said you couldn't go with me and Mommy if they made us leave. You have yellow."

"Katie, it's okay."

"No!" she screamed. "It's not. I want you to be with us."

"I'll catch up."

She shook her head. "Promise not to get mad."

168

"Why am I going to get mad?" Lev asked.

She unzipped the pink bookbag, reached in and pulled out a green band. "Large. Bottom drawer. So it will fit." She extended it out to Lev.

She had stolen an immunity band.

Before Lev could react, I quickly grabbed the one on his arm, pulled it apart and snatched the one from her hand. I snapped it onto him.

"There. Let's go," I said.

"This is dishonest, Nila."

"Fuck that," I told him then turned to Katie and mouthed the words, "Thank you." I reached down and lifted her.

"Let me." Lev took Katie from me and I swore he paused to give a grateful hug to my child.

It was hard for me to walk, especially down the stairs. It was obvious we were the last ones out of the building.

As we walked out, the street was jammed packed. People crowded, squished in so tight it sucked the air. And they moved, slowly, like a wave that grabbed us and brought us along. Every person tried to get ahead of the one in front. The sirens continuously blasted and along with the emotional cries of people, it was so loud.

"Please keep moving," a voice on speaker announced. "Yellow move north down St Paul to the mall. Blue and green move south to Smally Park."

Were they serious? No wonder it was a jam. They had everyone moving in different directions.

I couldn't see anything. Backs, heads. I kept standing on tip toes to find Ben, calling out his name.

"Ben! Ben!"

"I saw him. He's down the street," Lev said. "This is insane. Not to mention dangerous."

169

"We can't even move," I said. "Do you still see him?"

Lev lifted his chin, he stood above most people and when I saw he was searching, I knew it wasn't good.

Lev shook his head.

"Fleck?"

"I don't see him."

"Oh my God."

"Hey. We have a plan. We'll find each other. Right now, I have to get us out. Hold on to me."

I grabbed his arm.

Lev turned and moved back against the grain, shoving through. I couldn't see anything, I just had to hold on and blindly follow.

It wasn't long before I knew where we were. Back at the apartment building.

"Lev?" I questioned.

"Trust me. I've been in this situation before. New York. People think inside the box." He grabbed the door handle to the apartment and opened it.

Just as I stepped inside, the sirens stopped.

It brought an immediate silence.

"You think it's over?" I asked. "False alarm."

I didn't need for Lev to answer me, the wave of panic and horrifying screams from people said it all.

Lev moved me inside and shut the door. He handed me Katie.

"Take her for a second, follow me." Lev stepped ahead and swung his bag around as he moved. I heard it unzipper, then Lev stopped walking.

"What are you doing?" I asked. "It's not safe in the building. Lev, they clean house."

"I know. We're not staying." He turned around handing me a piece of paper that was wrinkled from folding. "Hold that." He took Katie. "We're headed to Smally Park." He started walking again.

I looked down. It was a map, the one that Sean had given us complete with a 'you are here' star.

"He gave that to us when we were close to that park."

"Where are we going, Lev?" I asked.

"Out the back door. When have you ever known me, Nila, to not look for the exits?" He turned a bend at the end of the hall and sure enough there was another door. "Let me see that map."

I held it up for him.

"Okay, we're going to go out this door. Go down two blocks and make a left. The park should be another block." He pushed the door open and looked. "Let's go."

We stepped out into a back alley. Only a few people ran down the street. We could still hear the screams carrying to us.

Lev picked up the pace and I tried so hard to keep up, but the more I walked, the more my hips ached. It was as if they were locking up. Finally, I gave in and told him I couldn't keep the pace.

He slowed down for me. When we reached the left turn we ran into the people again, though nowhere near the amount that was on Main Street. All moved fast and in the same direction, probably for Smally park.

That many people were immune? I thought the number of immune was small. It was when I caught a glimpse of a band or two as people ran by me, that I knew they were just trying to get out. To get on one of the buses or whatever vehicle they were using to evacuate us.

We weren't near the end of the crowd of people, somewhere in the middle. I could hear engines revving and vehicles driving off. As we got closer, I saw taillights as bus after bus rolled out. Most not from the park.

Finally, I saw one lone bus. Just one. A gray school bus.

A man's voice shouted out, "Blue and green first, then we'll take yellow. Blue and green."

It seemed so far away. I felt desperate. We weren't getting out.

And just as I started to fall deep into a state of despair, I was overwhelmed with gratefulness that Lev was so tall. He hoisted Katie above his head and shouted. I didn't recall ever hearing him so loud. His voice boomed out, "She is a blue! She's a blue."

"Let him through!" the man replied. "Let them through." He fired his weapon once in the air.

It quieted the people down, brought a pause of stillness and after bringing Katie back to his arms, Lev grabbed my hand and plowed through.

We made it.

"Bands," the man, a soldier, said. His name, Hawkins, was on the front of his uniform.

He checked Katie's, then mine, then finally Lev. He waved us on. "Go on."

There were only about ten people on the bus. Not one face I recognized. I looked at wrists and bands as I walked by, all of them green.

Lev led us to the back—I suppose to be nearer to an exit—and we all squeezed in one seat.

The second I sat down, I caught my breath and squeezed Lev's hand.

"We did it, we're getting out," Lev said.

"What about Ben and Sawyer?" Katie asked.

"I bet they're already on a bus," Lev said. "They were far ahead of us."

I glanced up watching the bus fill quickly.

I heard Hawkins call out, "That's it. That's all."

He stepped back on the bus, but before he could, people rushed it, racing on despite his best efforts to close the door.

"Go," Hawkins said to the driver. "Go now."

Door still open, people trying to board, hanging on, the bus took off.

It drove quickly, though not as fast as I would have hoped. I turned to look out the back window, watching as the taillights illuminated the people running for us and those lying on the ground after being dropped from the bus.

The lights from Colony One were growing further in the distance. It then dawned on me: we didn't close the fence and those people were running aimlessly through an unprotected area.

Somehow I had a hunch, a painful gut instinct that it was going to happen.

There was a reason for such a hurried and immediate evacuation. It wasn't just a breach, it was much more.

Too many infected and deaders.

They came from both sides of the road attacking the unsuspecting people.

I closed my eyes and faced forward.

"Nila?" Lev called my name with a question.

"The infected," I said.

"We'll be at the receiving center shortly. That's fenced in. We'll be safe," he said. "We'll wait for Ben, Sawyer, and Fleck." He grabbed my hand.

We were rolling and moving smoothly, halfway there. I could see a bus in front of us not that far away.

Maybe Ben and Sawyer were on that bus.

I sat back to relax, to absorb my safe status, when a bang rang out. It was followed by a thump as something smashed against the windshield. The bus bounced as if we'd run over something, and with

173

a loud squeal of the brakes we swerved left and right until we finally stopped.

People screamed.

"Quiet," Hawkins shouted, then turned to the driver.

"We blew a tire when we hit them," the driver said.

"Can you ride on the rim?" Hawkins asked. "We're close. There are too many of them for us to walk. We have another mile. We have to go another mile."

"I'll try."

The bus started moving.

Hawkins tilted his head to the radio on his collar. He said something about how much time, or how long and I turned to look back.

We weren't moving fast enough. In fact we were barely moving.

Floor it, please floor it, I begged in my mind.

They were coming. A group of them. They raced at top speed for the bus and I could tell by their relentless running they were infected.

If we stopped, even for a second, they would be on us.

Faster, please faster.

Maybe I was imagining how close they were. Maybe it was my fear.

Then suddenly my fear of the infected was replaced with something else.

At the same time Hawkins shouted out, "Everyone get down! Away from the windows!" I saw the dots of lights in the sky above Colony One.

"Nila! Down!" Lev charged.

Katie was already on the floor. I was able to crouch down on the floor part way in the aisle. I knew there was no way for Lev to fit.

174

I felt his weight above us. Did he just lie down on the seat? Was he hovering above us? I didn't know.

I reached for my child and my eyes connected with her as I grabbed her arm and gave it a squeeze. It was comforting to see the look in her eyes. She wasn't scared, and in that moment, I took strength from her.

I knew whatever happened, we were together, and we had tried.

TWENTY-FIVE

CONTINGENCY

June 20

Five explosions rang out and every window on the bus exploded. It filled with an intense heat and I hated the thought that my last moments would be touching my daughter as we were burned alive.

That didn't happen.

We survived.

The bus, however, was undriveable, and we had to walk that last mile to the safety of the receiving center.

It was the longest mile I had ever walked.

Every step I took I kept looking out. Looking back at the dark smoke that lingered over Colony One. We were in a wide-open area, vulnerable to any infected. Nowhere to run or to hide.

Fifty people walking the road together.

We were a mobile buffet.

But there were no infected, at least none that came for us.

When we stepped through the gates that surrounded the receiving center, I could see the station wagon still parked, right where we left it.

When we first got to the receiving center nearly two weeks earlier, there was barely anyone there. Now it was packed, every square inch.

I was hopeful that we would find Ben, Sawyer or Fleck. I kept looking at the wagon, expecting to see one of them waiting. There were so many people so we waited outside watching every bus as they loaded them to take survivors to another Colony.

They weren't there.

Evacuation buses went all directions, north, south, and west. We were told there was another receiving center to the northwest, and they could have been there.

We stayed at the receiving center another day. We didn't want to leave or take the only transportation for Ben and Fleck.

However, no one else from Colony One came and we were among the last remaining. Though we weren't the only ones waiting for someone.

When it was time to go, to give up the wait, there were only a handful of us from Colony One, a few soldiers and a worker or two, that remained.

The receiving center was deemed closed.

Colony One...dead.

We used the facilities to clean up and stock up, then relying on our 'if we ever get separated' plan, we loaded into the station wagon for our meet-up destination of Cobb Corner.

A woman named Meg, along with her nine-year-old daughter ended up joining us. They had nowhere else to go and didn't trust the Colony living.

They were scared and traumatized and said very little on the ride. It took Katie's constant prodding to get the girl to speak.

After two overnight stops, three days in the car, they were chatting away by the time we reached the border of Virginia.

The fueling and help stops we saw on the way to Colony One were now few and far between. They were withdrawing. The last one gave us as much as they could in canisters that we carried on the luggage rack.

I didn't worry though. We always found means to get gas, at least while the gas was good.

We took our time, we felt battered both emotionally and physically.

When we were within a hundred-mile range of Cobb Corner, we started attempts on the radio. It had charged enough from the car ride, and I prayed that Westin and Cobb Corner were alright.

"Cobb Corner come in, please come in."

Every ten miles.

"Cobb Corner, come in, are you there. Come in."

Finally, with twenty-two miles to go we made contact.

"This is Cobb Corner, is that you, Nila?" Westin's voice called out.

I brought the transceiver to my mouth. "Yes, yes, it is. Westin?"

"My God, you're alive. Hold on."

I looked at Lev. "Did he just tell me to hold on?"

Lev smiled. A tired smile, he looked worn down.

After a few minutes, the radio crackled. "Hey, what the heck is taking you guys so long?"

I wanted to scream with excitement. "Fleck!"

"Yep. Here waiting on you. Thought maybe you and the big guy said screw it and went to the cabin."

Lev took the radio. "I wanted to. Hey, Fleck. We couldn't find Ben and Sawyer."

"That's because they're here. I got here first, they got here yesterday. I'll tell you all about our great escape when you get here."

"I look forward to it," Lev said. "See you soon."

Instantly, a renewed energy hit the car. Especially for Lev, Katie and me. They made it. We didn't lose them. Soon enough, all of us would be together. I couldn't wait to see them and more so Bella and Christian.

Invigored by the knowledge that we hadn't failed, that we had all survived, the remaining miles to Cobb Corner were good ones. We couldn't get there fast enough.

When we rounded the bend into Cobb Corner, I had forgotten that it was a subsidiary of sorts for The Colony. More than likely that was how Fleck and Ben ended up there. I remembered Clare telling me they were going to send people there.

They hadn't erected a safety fence, but there was a checkpoint just at the edge of town. It wasn't as scary as before: the armed guards only wore facial masks instead of hazmat suits.

Ben, Sawyer, Fleck, Bella, the baby, and Westin were all waiting for us. A welcoming committee that was a sight for sore eyes.

We stopped right at the checkpoint. Katie jumped from the car and raced toward the group.

The guard stopped her. "Hold on little one, let me scan you."

He did and gave her the all clear, and Katie ran to Fleck. I didn't think she liked him that much. Yet, she hugged him so tight.

"Go on," I told Meg. "Please. You'll like it here. I'll introduce you."

Meg held her daughter's hand and walked toward the guard. I looked back to see Lev at the hatch of the wagon.

"What are you doing?" I asked. "Leave it. We can get our stuff later."

"Okay." He shut the hatch.

I waited for him and together we walked to the guard.

He stopped me first with his scanner. First my face, head to the left, head to the right, then my hands...clear.

Lev stepped forward. I waited, inching my way forward to greet our friends, happy to see that they were fine.

I can only imagine how big the smile was on my face. My cheeks hurt.

I heard the guard with Lev. "Face forward."

Beep.

"Head to the left."

Beep.

"Head to the right."

Beep.

Then the scary sound.

The sound of engaging weapons.

I spun around to see the rifles aimed at Lev.

"No!" I screamed out, racing forward. "Don't shoot. Don't you shoot him!" I lunged with everything I had, bodily blocking him. "What the fuck?" I spat, out of breath and confused with emotions. "What the fuck are you doing?" I pulled out my pistol and aimed it directly at the guard's head. "Don't you fucking shoot."

Within a second, Fleck was blocking Lev and Ben joined in.

"Ma'am, step back. The scan showed…"

"I don't care what the scan showed. You're gonna shoot him?"

"Nila," Lev spoke calmly. "Put the gun down."

"I will do no such thing," I argued.

"Soldier," Ben stepped forward. "I'm a doctor. Scan him again."

"But it showed…"

Then Ben blasted, "Scan him again!"

I held my aim steady as he lifted the scanner again.

Ben walked forward standing beside the man as he scanned Lev.

He scanned his face.

Head to the left.

Head to the right.

And I saw Ben's eyes.

My world crumbled.

There was no mistake.

Somehow, someway, the virus hit home again.

Lev…was infected.

TWENTY-FIVE

FROM LEV'S SIDE

Nila always had the ability to bring out every emotion in me. Standing in that street, the guard in front of me, the scanner in his hand, Nila brought forth a feeling of utter devastation. I didn't feel it for myself, I felt it for her.

I never in my entire life wanted to hurt her. Ever. But I did. I saw it. I instantly broke her heart.

Nila was strong. The strongest person I knew.

Yet, she lost it. She physically crumbled, dropped to her knees crying out, "No, do it again. Do it again."

"Nila, please." I reached for her. "Nila."

She slowly swung her head my way. Her eyes glossed over and she grabbed my hand.

"Not you, Lev, please not you."

"It's okay." I pulled on her hand to get her to stand. "It's okay." Then I brought her into my arms.

It wasn't just her.

Ben's head lowered, he stared at the ground. He wouldn't even look at me. I could hear Fleck behind me repeatedly saying, "Oh my God. Oh my God.'

And Katie.

She rushed over and clung to my legs.

Did she even understand? I wasn't sure I did.

How?

How was I even infected? Was I near someone? I could think about it all I wanted, but it didn't matter; though I felt fine, I wouldn't for long.

Rules were rules and because Westin and Cobb Corner agreed to be part of the Colonies, all infected, no matter what stage would be eliminated.

I was to be like those people on the street in the small town.

Executed without trial.

I got it. I did. I carried the virus and I was a threat to anyone who wasn't immune. Thank God, the person I loved most in the world wouldn't catch it from me. I always suspected she had some sort of immunity. When her daughter Addy was dying, Nila never left her side. Never stopped touching or holding her.

I suppose the soldier didn't want to shoot me with a child clinging to my legs and while I held Nila in my arms.

Then again, he wasn't quite happy that Nila put a gun to his head.

Not that the shock wore off, but it lessened some enough for Nila to turn from my hold and face the soldier.

"Please don't shoot him," she said softly.

"Ma'am, I am sorry. I'm not a killer, this is not what I want to do. I don't enjoy it," he said. "But he is under Colony Law in Cobb Corner."

Westin's voice cut through as he spoke up. "But he's not in Cobb Corner. Not yet." He stepped forward. "Cobb Corner starts at Mack's Pharmacy. I made that agreement. The pharmacy is right there." Westin pointed a half a block from us. "So you're off the hook."

The soldier stepped back.

"Lev." Ben approached me. "We can fight this. We can. I'll do what I did for Corbin. I'll blast you with anti-viral medication, every kind I can find at that pharmacy."

I nodded, but I knew better. Corbin was a special breed. He was like Katie.

"Is the pharmacy still stocked?" Ben asked Westin.

Westin nodded. "Yeah, so is Bilkos in the next town. We haven't had a doctor."

"Good. Good. I'll be right back." Ben walked up to Westin. They exchanged some words but I couldn't hear what they were saying. When they walked off, they didn't go to the pharmacy.

"I'm sorry, Nila," I told her.

"What? Don't apologize. Please." She drew in a breath and I could hear it shiver as she did. After staring at me for a few seconds, she wiped her hand over her face, sniffed hard and pulled her shoulders back. "Okay. Alright." She exhaled in a huff. "Give me a second." She stepped back, hands on hips and pivoted left to right, looking up and down. While someone that didn't know her would think she was insane or losing it, I knew Nila. She was pulling it together.

It was only a couple minutes of standing there in silence, absorbing the reality, when Ben returned.

"I wanted to talk to you before I went to the pharmacy," Ben said. "Westin connected me with The Colony. I don't have a lot of experience with the illness form of this thing. Only the form from bites. So they told me, as you're not symptomatic, only scan confirmed, it'll be another two days before your symptoms hit. Progression with this illness is four days to phase. Or—"

"I know," I cut him off. "I know what that means."

"So we hit you now with everything we can," Ben said.

Nila turned to him. "Do it now, please. And get everything we need. Everything." She then walked to Fleck. "Can you check the wagon for me? Check the oil, everything, tires. Make sure it's good."

"Yeah, absolutely."

Nila walked to the wagon, I could tell by the way she moved she was in some sort of survival mode. She opened the passenger door, reached in for something, stepped back, and closed the door again. She spread a map on the hood.

Fleck leaned in joining her. Holding Katie's hand, I walked over.

"What's going on?" I asked.

She rambled quickly as if in an out loud thinking mode. "This thing got us about four hundred miles per tank on the way back here. Three hundred first trip. Of course that was all back roads. Highway's pretty clear now. Almost a straight shot. We just saw that. Eighteen-gallon tank. Got a quarter tank left. One canister on the luggage rack." She spun to Fleck.

"So you only need maybe another canister? Two to be safe?" Fleck asked.

"Yes," she said.

"We'll get it."

"Mommy?" Katie called her. "What are you talking about?"

Nila faced me. She smiled at Katie then glanced to me. "We're only about four hundred or so miles. Not that far, not that long." She looked at her watch. "It's ten now. If we go straight through, only stop to gas up, we'll get there before dark."

"Where are we going, Nila?" I asked.

"Where do you think, Lev? To the cabin," she said. "We're going home."

TWENTY-SIX

RETREAT

When we left home, even the first time in search of The Green, Lev had said he never wanted to leave. He had repeatedly said he wanted to go back, that it was the place to be. How unfair it would be if we didn't return to the cabin one last time.

I saw it in his face when I told him. He was happy.

It took everything I had to be strong. To not crumble into a million pieces. My heart was broken. I could already feel the ache in my chest when I thought about losing him. I dreaded if that day actually came.

I saw what the infection looked like. I saw it was there when I watched the soldier scan Lev again. The veins at the bottom of his neck were black, but only with the special light of the scanner.

It sickened me.

Leaving Cobb Corner was the best choice I could make for us. It was the right choice, even if he were allowed in Cobb.

So, Lev, Katie, and I packed up for yet another road trip. But we had an additional passenger this time.

Bella had made a friend in Cobb Corner and suggested we bring him for Katie. To keep her occupied and her mind busy. Nothing would be better for Katie while she faced the prospect of losing Lev.

A three-year-old Beagle named Caesar. He wasn't a big dog, nor small, he was the perfect size. And Bella was right, he was what we needed. He had survived the outbreak even when his owner turned. He handled the car ride better than me.

When we left The Colony we had taken Interstate 81. We knew The Colony was pulling out and the one fuel place that was still there was far passed the turn we made to jump on the Pennsylvania Turnpike.

We looped around the city of Pittsburgh; it had been the easiest road trip yet. It was a blessing and a gift, and we were back at the cabin long before the sun even set.

Lev had driven the last leg of the trip. We had secured the fence when we left. It hadn't been that long and nothing had changed except the grass was long.

He had a huge peaceful smile on his face when we stopped the car in the driveway.

Katie excitedly jumped out. "Come on, Caesar." After a single bark, the dog followed.

Katie immediately ran through the high grass, playing with her new friend.

"See?" Lev said. "She wanted to come back too."

I don't know why, but Lev felt the need to mow the grass immediately after we'd unpacked. I guess a part of me attributed the virus to a bedridden person. He wasn't sick, not yet. Ben estimated that he didn't get it at The Colony—he caught it somewhere, somehow, on the way back to Cobb Corner. The timing would suggest that.

He loaded Lev up with anti-viral medication, pain medication, and then one final dose. The syringe that contained enough medication that Lev would go in peace, if that time came.

I couldn't chance Lev turning. I would never want that for him and there was no way I could handle him if he did turn.

I prayed, every second and every moment I got, I prayed that he wouldn't get sick.

Please God, let it work.

The first night home, after Katie was tucked in bed, Caesar beside her, Lev and I sat on the porch. That wide top step that I loved to share with him.

We drank warm beer and sipped on shots.

"Thank you for this," Lev said. "This is perfect."

"Yeah, it is."

He grabbed my hand and held it between both of his. "It's hard to believe, you know, that this is real."

"I don't believe it yet. I refuse."

"We can always hope, right?"

I nodded.

"But..."

"Lev, please don't."

"No, Nila listen to me. If I do get sick. I don't want to do it in some bed. I don't want you or Katie to see me like that."

"You sound like my father," I said.

"He was wise man. A good man."

I looked at him. "He passed away in that recliner."

"He passed where he wanted to go and did so on his terms," Lev said. "Before he got too sick."

"Are you saying that's what you want?"

Lev bit his bottom lip in hesitation. "It is."

"So you want me to give up on you before we see if Ben's treatment is going to work?"

"Corbin was immune, we know that. I'm not."

"You don't know..."

188

"I do know," Lev said strongly. "And if the time comes, I will choose how and where."

"You want to go to Big Bear," I said.

"What? No. Right here. Right here. Like this."

"You want to die on our front porch?"

"If it's not too much for you. I want it just like this. With you."

"I won't leave your side, Lev." I blocked out my emotions and coughed them away. "But, you know, it's not gonna happen. You're fine. You'll be fine."

TWENTY-SEVEN

FIRST STEP, LAST STEP

June 24

I was wrong. I didn't see it so I refused to believe it, but sooner than we thought, it hit him. After the first night in the cabin, Lev woke up fevered. He fought it, pretended he was fine, but his face was so pale, and those black spiderweb veins crept up the right side of his neck. He lacked energy, but he pushed forward.

By the third day of being home, he couldn't push forward any longer. He couldn't keep anything down, not even water, but he tried.

We sat all morning and afternoon on the porch watching Katie play with Caesar.

He was so sick. I just wanted to hold him, take it all away, but I couldn't.

"You know," Lev said. "You hated dogs."

"No, I did not. I hated taking care of them," I said. "Remember. Bobby would ask for a pet and I got stuck cleaning up after him."

"Oh, yeah, that's true. I'm glad you brought the dog."

"Me too."

"What are you going to do?"

"What do you mean?"

"I won't be here much…"

"Lev, stop."

"I need to know, Nila," Lev said. "I need to know. Okay?"

"I'm staying. Right here. Me and Katie for the time being."

"Alone. You won't be afraid?"

"Not at all. We have enough wood for the winter. I can hunt. We'll be good. I can take care of us." I lifted my head to the sound of a motor.

Lev started to stand.

"Stay put." I pulled out my pistol as a car pulled up. Caesar started barking out of control. "Katie, come back to the cabin."

The car stopped at the gate and the driver's side opened.

Ben stepped out and unlocked the gate. He waved.

I could feel it on my face, the muscles tensing fighting back any tears.

When they pulled in and unloaded, it took everything I had not to break down with gratefulness.

Fleck, Bella, the baby, Sawyer and the new woman Meg, and her daughter.

They all unloaded.

I set down the pistol on the step and raced to Ben, hugging him. "You came. Thank you."

"We couldn't stay away." Ben pulled back and placed his hand on my face. "Something about his place. How is he?"

I shook my head. "It's fast. Too fast. It's almost time."

His hand slid from my face and he walked toward Lev. Fleck gave my hand a squeeze as he passed me and Bella wrapped her arms around me.

I stood back watching as they approached Lev.

He would never admit it, but Lev needed them.

He needed us all, just like we needed him.

"Do you think Grandma Lisa has a bottle of whiskey in heaven?" Katie asked Lev. "I wonder if she does."

Her comment made me cringe and laugh over dinner. A meal that was good for the soul as well as the belly. They had fun at my expense telling Lev how bad they felt for him eating my cooking for the past three days.

He actually joked and said he didn't notice because he couldn't keep it down.

But that moment was a ruse. A smoke screen to cover the inevitable.

"It's time," Ben told me. "We can't. He knows it. I know it. It's taking everything he has to keep his head up. As much as we want it, he's not coming back from this."

I hated to hear it, but I knew the words to be true.

It killed me to see Lev so sick.

He was ready. I had to be.

There were no drawn out goodbyes as we went to the porch. It was like it always was, them saying good night before he and I took our evening spot.

There was one difference. Katie hugged him and told him she loved him.

We closed the door behind us and sat down on the porch step. I had to help Lev because his balance was off.

My hands shook so bad as I held the syringe. It brought back painful memories of my father and of Addy. Lev had been there for me when Addy died. He did what I couldn't, giving her peace in her final stages. I had to be able to do that for him.

"Here." His hand lay over mine. "I'll do it."

"No. No. I'll do it," I told him. "I want to. Not that, you know, I want to but…"

"I get it."

I took a deep breath through my nostrils. "It'll be fast, Lev, you know that, right? Are you ready for this?"

"No, I'm not. But I don't want to go any further. The last thing I want is to turn. So please. I'm as ready as I'll ever be." He rolled up his sleeve.

Shaking, I brought the syringe to him and stopped. I placed my hand on his face and kissed him. "I love you. You know that right."

His facial muscles tightened and he nodded. "I do. I love you, too."

I couldn't look. I allowed for my fingers to feel his fevered flesh, and while looking at him, I injected the needle. His eyes closed when I plunged the medication into him.

"I'm sorry," I whispered.

"Don't be." His shoulders heaved back in a breath, then he scooted from me. I wondered for a moment what he was doing, until he leaned sideways, placing his head on my lap. "Thank you for this, Nila. Thank you for everything."

"No, Lev, thank you."

He was tired and sick and I think...I think he was done. He was finished. His arms gripped my legs like a pillow as my hand rested on his head.

I felt like I should have been talking, telling him things, sharing stories, but I couldn't talk. Every time I tried to speak, my throat closed up. I choked on my emotions.

My mind said it, I thought.

I love you Lev, so much. You have been there for me my entire life. Nothing will ever fill this void. Nothing. This is unfair. So unfair.

For decades I had known him and loved him and now he was leaving me.

Every thought I had caused another tear to fall down my face. As my fingers ran through his hair, I tried to hide the sluggish sniffles that built, tried to stop the tears. It was impossible.

I couldn't say when he left me, but he did. When his grip on my legs released, I imagined he'd fallen asleep.

Sometime during the course of the night, probably not long after we sat on the porch, Lev passed away.

I didn't acknowledge it until morning when Ben came out. I was still holding him, not wanting to move.

I didn't want to let go. I couldn't let go.

It was Lev. The moment he and Fleck lifted him from my lap, the pain punched a hole in my heart. I was gutted emotionally. I had to turn away when they carried him. I couldn't see his lifeless body.

It was hard enough to breathe, let alone move. And I didn't. I stayed on our porch until I could try to process it.

But processing the loss of Lev was something I would never be able to do.

TWENTY-EIGHT

HOME

July 12

It was the first warm day of the summer. It had only been a couple weeks since Lev had died and I was nowhere near myself. I wouldn't be for a while. Katie was sad, but she handled it like I thought she would. With a strength that I envied.

At the onset of the outbreak, when we had retreated to the cabin, we buried my husband in a spot behind the shed. That area grew into a cemetery. My husband, daughter, father, stepmother, brother. It was insane how many people I loved were there. How many people I loved who had died from the virus. I hated the virus. We all did. What started as one grave, turned into many. I never would have believed it. Each grave had a white cross made by Lev. A year earlier, during the turmoil when we briefly lost the cabin to that gang, they desecrated it.

It had been the first order of business when we returned from Cobb Corner. Lev fixed that cemetery.

It was only fitting that he not only be buried there but was given a cross as well.

We buried him next to his father, creating another row. I hoped we'd never have to put another person there.

Then again, I'd had that hope before.

It was hard to look at the cemetery. Occasionally I would glance at it, walk by, feeling the thump in my chest and flip of my stomach.

195

Hating the loss and wishing for the sadness to just go away. Katie visited it daily and had conversations. She showed Lev her drawings. For the time being I avoided it. If I didn't look, it wasn't real.

Every day I would walk out to the front and watch the gate, almost as if waiting for Lev to show up.

Deep in thought, standing at my spot in the driveway staring out, I jumped a little when Ben's hand tapped my shoulder.

"Sorry, didn't mean to scare you," he said.

"It's okay. Just thinking."

"How are you doing?"

"I'm doing. Trying…you know. It's tough."

"Oh, I know. I have been there. So…" Ben said with an exhale. "Fleck talk to you about going hunting?"

"Hunting? No." I shook my head.

"He wants to go out in an hour."

"Little late in the day for good hunting. Wait. Animals or infected?"

"Deaders. Saw a whole group by the Costco. I think it might be good for you to go."

"You're probably right."

"I am," Ben said. "Doctor's orders."

"Then I must follow." I folded my arms.

"Nila, you are a strong woman. Probably stronger than you realize. Lev knew that. He's counting on you to be okay, you know."

"Yeah, I know. And I will be."

"I know you will." He gave a squeeze to my shoulder. "I'll tell Fleck."

I nodded and after he walked away, I thought about what he said. How Lev was counting on me to be okay. It was an odd phrasing of words, considering I had counted on Lev for everything, especially after the outbreak.

Lev left this earth believing I was strong enough to carry on. I was. I just had to get there. I would and could because I had my daughter and my friends. I had so much reason.

I would take it one day at a time, one step at a time, and I was at the best place possible to do so: the cabin.

We were where Lev wanted us to be.

We were home.

ABOUT THE AUTHOR

Jacqueline Druga is a native of Pittsburgh, PA. Her works include genres of all types but she favors post-apocalypse and apocalypse writing.

For updates on new releases you can find the author on:

Facebook: @jacquelinedruga

Twitter: @gojake

www.jacquelinedruga.com

Made in the USA
Columbia, SC
10 July 2022